"What's going on, Valentin?" I demanded, forcing the husky sound from my voice. **"Why am I here? I have to get back to Madrid."**

"You're not going back to Madrid." He didn't smile this time, his hand dropping away. "You're not marrying him, Olivia. I forbid it."

"What do you mean you forbid it?" I stared at him in outrage as he turned away, going back out onto the deck to grab the white towel that had been laid across a white lounge chair.

"You heard me." He dried himself off with brisk strokes, then casually draped the towel around his neck, gripping the ends in his large, long-fingered hands, still making no effort whatsoever to hide his nakedness. "You can't marry him. I won't let you."

"You...won't *let* me?" For a minute all I could do was blink in astonishment at his arrogance, his sheer audacity. "As I recall, no one died and made you king."

Amusement glittered in his eyes. "There's still time."

Rival Billionaire Tycoons

Dark-hearted brothers set on vengeance!

Valentin and Constantine Silvera were once each other's only support under their cruel father's rule. But the circumstances of their childhood drove an irreparable wedge between them and ultimately drove Valentin to escape in the only way he could imagine: by faking his own death.

Now Valentin is back, and he's on a mission to reclaim his inheritance. But neither of these hard-hearted billionaires are backing down! It will take the women they are destined for to show them there's more to life than power and control...and perhaps even to reunite them.

Read Valentin's story in
A Diamond for My Forbidden Bride
Available now!

And look out for Constantine's story
Stolen for My Spanish Secret
Coming soon!

Jackie Ashenden

A DIAMOND FOR MY
FORBIDDEN BRIDE

ISBN-13: 978-1-335-56968-4

A Diamond for My Forbidden Bride

Harlequin Enterprises ULC
22 Adelaide St. West, 41st Floor
Toronto, Ontario M5H 4E3, Canada
www.Harlequin.com

Printed in U.S.A.

Jackie Ashenden writes dark, emotional stories with alpha heroes who've just gotten the world to their liking only to have it blown apart by their kick-ass heroines. She lives in Auckland, New Zealand, with her husband, the inimitable Dr. Jax, two kids and two rats. When she's not torturing alpha males and their gutsy heroines, she can be found drinking chocolate martinis, reading anything she can lay her hands on, wasting time on social media or being forced to go mountain biking with her husband. To keep up-to-date with Jackie's new releases and other news, sign up to her newsletter at jackieashenden.com.

Books by Jackie Ashenden

Harlequin Presents

The Italian's Final Redemption
The World's Most Notorious Greek
The Innocent Carrying His Legacy
The Wedding Night They Never Had
The Innocent's One-Night Proposal

Pregnant Princesses

Pregnant by the Wrong Prince

Visit the Author Profile page
at Harlequin.com for more titles.

This one's for Ella.

CHAPTER ONE

Olivia

A MAN WAS leaning in the doorway that led to the upper floors of the Silvera mansion and, even though his face was in shadow, his head was turned in my direction and I could tell he was watching me.

I could feel the pressure of his gaze like ghostly fingers trailing down my spine.

A shiver whispered across my skin.

I couldn't make out his features, since he was leaning just out of the light, but I could see already that he was tall and broad-shouldered and powerful.

Unease coiled inside me.

Security had been tight for Domingo Silvera's funeral and it was even tighter here in Madrid, at the Silvera mansion, for his wake.

But, given Domingo's fame, how could it not be? He'd been the CEO of Silver Incorporated, one of Europe's biggest companies, with shares in tech, R&D, manufacturing, finance—you name it, Silver Inc probably had a stake in it. It was a behemoth, making more than a few governments give it a sideways look.

Domingo's father, Diego, who'd inherited the family traits of ruthlessness and arrogance from the ancient line of Spanish aristocrats they were descended from, had started the company nearly a hundred years earlier, and since then it had grown and prospered. Yet it hadn't been until Domingo had taken over that it had flourished to become the massive company it was today.

Many people had come this evening and the ornate marbled ballroom of the mansion was full of politicians, business people, heads of state, the rich and the famous…all here to pay their respects to one of Europe's most powerful men.

Even Domingo's rivals and enemies, of which there were many, were here.

Perhaps that man in the doorway was one of them. An enemy come to gloat over the corpse of a dead foe. What else could explain the aura of menace I'd felt emanating from him?

Normally I'd never let something as basic as unease get to me, but I still shivered yet again, and found myself shifting closer to my fiancé, Constantine Silvera. He was Domingo's son, heir to all Domingo's power, and was now newly crowned CEO of Silver Inc.

I didn't need his protection, but he was tall and powerfully built, and radiated a certain reassurance that in the moment some part of me craved.

Constantine was cold, arrogant, ferociously intelligent, a wolf when it came to business and frightened people just as his father had. All those aristocratic traits had been distilled in him and he used them to his advantage. Ruthlessly.

He was also the possessor of the famous Silvera beauty—black hair, black eyes and the kind of profile that would have looked good on a coin. He'd been named for an emperor and an emperor he was. One that didn't bother with the velvet glove. There was only the iron fist.

So, yes, I should have felt safe with him in a mansion surrounded by the tightest security on the planet.

I was the CEO of Wintergreen Fine Diamonds, my family's old and illustrious jewel company, and had a fairly powerful security team of my own, all of whom were present tonight.

Yet I didn't feel reassured.

Constantine was probably deciding when the appropriate time was to give his speech, thanking everyone for coming and so on. If he noticed my uneasiness, he gave no sign, his cold, black eyes surveying the guests dispassionately.

Usually nothing could get past the façade of cool competence and poise that I'd cultivated over the years. I'd had to. Being a female CEO of a very traditional company required a certain strength and I didn't like anything to undermine it.

Things such as the shadowy presence of a stranger.

Constantine would be appalled if he knew. He saw my icy calm as strong, and strength was a quality he admired, as he so often told me.

Though, ours wasn't a love match.

My own father had died eighteen months earlier, leaving behind him a legacy of terrible financial mismanagement that could have resulted in Wintergreen going bankrupt. It had come as a terrible shock, since I'd always seen him as the consummate businessman. So had the board, and they'd been very clear that they didn't want me at the helm. It had been a…testing time. Then the past had come calling unexpectedly in the shape of Constantine Silvera.

I knew him from years ago, when I was a child and our families would holiday on the same Caribbean island. While there had been… difficulties back then, that was all water under the bridge now.

He'd said he'd heard about Wintergreen's financial issues and that he'd like to help. He'd been prepared to help me, to pay my father's debts and get the company solvent again as long as he took over management of it until the company was on its feet again. Oh, yes, and in return all he'd required was my hand in marriage. He needed heirs, it was time and he'd always appreciated the Wintergreen genes.

Initially I'd been suspicious of his offer. The board already thought I was unsuitable to take over Wintergreen, since they were all traditionalists who didn't like a woman managing the company. Having Constantine take over management for a time would make me look weak, as would marrying him.

Then again, if I wanted the company to survive, accepting Constantine's offer had been the best way forward. Also, there was another plus: children.

Wintergreen was a family company, and if I wanted it to remain so I would need heirs, just as Constantine would. My father had always said that I could be CEO of Wintergreen or be a mother but I couldn't be both, and that when I had children I would have to step down.

He had generally been right about most things when it had come to running Wintergreen but, given his financial mismanagement, I'd begun to question a few things.

I didn't see why I should have to have to step down from being CEO, for example. I wanted a child, I wanted to be head of Wintergreen and Constantine could definitely give me that.

I'd been told by my doctor that I had a limited window in which to get pregnant, and if I wanted children I had to start now, so it was that in the end that swayed me.

Also, there were worse things than having children with a physically perfect specimen of manhood who also just happened to be one of the most powerful men in Europe. His family history, of course, left a lot to be desired, which might not have made him the best choice to be the father of my children, but I could make it work. The child would have me, after all.

So I hadn't refused, I'd accepted, and here I was—his fiancée.

'Something the matter, Olivia?' Constantine's deep, cold voice tinged with the soft, musical Spanish accent he hadn't quite been able to get rid of jolted me. 'You seem disturbed.'

So, it seemed he *had* noticed my discomfort after all. How irritating.

I was excellent at projecting the kind of cool strength required of a CEO, but the fact that

Constantine had noticed my discomfort meant my usual veneer was slipping.

I didn't like that. He wasn't a man who invited deep confidences—not that I'd have felt comfortable sharing them with him even if he had been—and had given me nothing but chilly courtesy for the past three months of our engagement.

I didn't trust him. He was pure predator, just like his father had been, and if there was one thing I'd learned in the last eighteen months in the boardroom it was that showing weakness of any kind in front of a man like him was a mistake.

'I'm fine,' I said coolly, trying not to glance at the dark figure in the doorway yet again. 'Only wondering when you were going to start the speeches.'

'In a minute.'

I looked up at him. He sounded distracted, which was unusual. Normally he was all razor-sharp focus, like a shark sniffing blood in the water. When he had a target or a goal, he pursued it relentlessly.

Now, though, with his black eyes sweeping over the crowds like a searchlight, it seemed the target wasn't his speech but something else.

Strange. Was he looking for someone? Perhaps it was Jenny, his stepsister, who'd promised to be there for the funeral yet hadn't turned up so far. Or perhaps he'd sensed the guy in the doorway too.

Whatever, he didn't seem to be bothered by it the way I was. Then again, Constantine had always seemed impervious to any feeling whatsoever. He was like a glacier—cold, glittering and perfect.

I'd known Constantine since I'd been seven years old, but we'd never been close, despite him only being a few years older than me. He'd been cold even then, more interested in his studies and doing whatever Domingo asked him to than playing games with Valentin and I...

Valentin.

An old, worn grief twisted inside me, a grief I thought I'd left behind a long time ago; the edges were somehow still sharp even after all these years.

How ridiculous. I shouldn't be thinking of him.

I forced my gaze away from the man I was going to marry, the man who was the mirror image of the boy I'd once loved with all of my poor, silly teenaged heart.

The boy who'd died in a car accident fifteen years ago.

He and Constantine were identical twins, and

many people had been unable to tell them apart, but never me. I'd always known who was who.

How can you marry him? When all you'll ever see is everything he's not? Everything you lost...

I ignored the thought. Really, I should stop listening to the ghost of my fifteen-year-old, overly dramatic self. I'd buried that weepy, hysterical child after Valentin had died and I'd moved on. I was nothing like her now and I didn't want to be.

Abruptly, Constantine stopping searching and nodded to one of his aides, who immediately called for everyone's attention.

The buzz of conversation died and I shoved away the echo of a long-ago grief, composing myself, turning myself back into the diamond heiress and Constantine Silvera's cool and poised fiancée.

'Friends,' Constantine began, the ice in his voice searing all the warmth from the word. 'Thank you all for coming. We are here today to celebrate the life of Domingo Silvera, my father—'

'That sounds like my cue.' The words were deep, gravelly, cutting through Constantine's speech like a hot knife through frozen butter.

A shocked silence fell as everyone in the

room turned and looked in the direction of the voice.

It had come from the man in the doorway.

A premonition gripped me, wrapping around my throat and twisting hard.

I had no idea where it had come from or why, but I suddenly knew without a doubt that something terrible was about to happen.

I opened my mouth to warn Constantine but, just at that moment, the man shoved himself away from the door frame and stepped out into the ballroom.

A ripple of sound passed around the room, a kind of gasp and sigh combined, and an abrupt, scorching heat swept over me.

That man… I knew him.

He strolled into the room with the powerful, predatory grace of a panther, his hands thrust casually in his pockets.

He was as tall as Constantine and as broad. He had the same strongly carved, fiercely beautiful face. The same straight nose, high cheekbones and hard, carved mouth. The same coal-black hair, black brows and deeply set black eyes.

Constantine's mirror image.

Yet there were some slight differences. This man's hair was slightly longer, grazing the collar of his white shirt, which he wore open with no tie, unlike Constantine. He didn't have Constantine's air of icy control, either. No, this man had the opposite.

He burned like a flame.

As suddenly as the heat had swept over me, it vanished, leaving behind it the freeze of a deep, echoing shock.

I'd only ever met one other man who burned like that, and he hadn't been a man, but a boy. And that boy was dead. He'd died long ago and I'd mourned him with everything in me.

Valentin Silvera, Constantine's twin.

My poise vanished. My fingers were blocks of ice, and so were my feet, and I could feel the same shock that gripped me wash through the assembled crowd. They were all staring at Constantine Silvera's duplicate, strolling calmly through their midst as if they weren't even there.

The man didn't look at the crowd. He looked only at Constantine, who didn't move or speak, as if he'd been turned to stone.

'Hello, little brother,' the man said in perfect, unaccented English. 'Long time, no see.'

The entire ballroom was utterly silent.

If I hadn't heard him speak, I'd have been certain I'd gone deaf.

'"Why are you here?" I hear you ask,' the man went on, even though no one had asked. No one had said a word. 'That's a good question and I'm glad you mentioned it.' He smiled, easily and friendly, but for the flames that leapt high in his eyes. 'I bet you'd forgotten, hadn't you, that I'm your elder by five minutes? Which of course makes me the oldest son.' He had a panther's smile, predatory and white. 'And, since I am, I'm going to claim the company, Constantine. Because you are not a fit man to run it.'

His smile widened and then his black gaze settled on me, burning far more fiercely than I remembered. Instead of the warm, comforting glow of a hearth fire, this was the wild heat of a forest blaze. 'Oh, yes, and that pretty fiancée of yours? You're not a fit man for her either, so she'll be mine too. Then again, she always was, remember?'

No, he couldn't be here.

He was dead. It had been a tragedy. A terrible tragedy. And I'd cried endless, dramatic tears at his funeral while Constantine had stood by the grave side, his face so pale it had looked as though it was carved from ice. And Domingo had been beside him, dominating the proceedings, a powerful, terrifying figure betraying no expression whatsoever. As if he hadn't just lost a son.

The silence in the room was deafening, not that I'd have heard anything anyway, over the blood roaring in my ears.

He wasn't dead, he was here, large as life and

radiating an aura of menace that the boy I remembered had never had.

A hundred times as gorgeous too.

The heart I'd thought I'd buried all those years ago suddenly shuddered to life in my chest, like an old machine starting up. It was beating so hard it felt as if it was going to break all my ribs.

Desperately, I curled my fingers into my palms, my nails digging in, trying to find my poise, my usual strength.

'What?' Valentin asked sardonically. 'Got nothing to say, Con? Don't worry, I'm sure you'll think of plenty tomorrow. Especially when my lawyers contact you.' His smile flickered like a flame. 'So, how would you like to play this? In full view of everyone? Or would you prefer to discuss this in private? Either is fine with me, though I have to tell you now, I do like an audience.'

I couldn't take my eyes off him. I couldn't breathe.

What was he doing here? What had happened to him? How was he alive? His body had been identified in the burned-out wreck of a car on the outskirts of Madrid. An accident, the police had determined.

There had been rumours he'd been trying to escape from Domingo, about whom rumours of violence had swirled, though everyone knew him to be a perfectly charming if arrogant kind of man. Rumours that perhaps it hadn't been entirely an accident.

And yet…he was here, right in front of me.

He hadn't been in that car, had he?

'You're dead.' Constantine's voice was a dark, icy wind, as if somehow saying the words would make Valentin's presence less real. 'You died fifteen years ago.'

Valentin's sardonic smile remained. 'Apparently reports of my death have been greatly exaggerated. As you can see.'

People were whispering, shock echoing and rebounding through the room.

I dug my nails harder into my palms, the cold seeping through me, unable to keep from staring at him, cataloguing all the changes the years had made.

He wasn't the same. I could see that now.

There had been a warmth to the boy I'd known and a calm patience I'd found so reassuring and steadying. My father had had no patience with my 'girlish tantrums', as he'd termed them, but Valentin had never minded.

We'd met on a secret beach on that Caribbean island and had become friends. And, as we'd grown older, we'd become something more.

He'd always had time for me. He'd always

been kind too, and funny. He hadn't seemed to care that I was only a girl.

But there was no trace of the boy in the man standing there with his hands in the pockets of his black trousers, his expression amused. He appeared casual and yet every line of him blazed with intensity.

He wasn't a flame now; he was a furnace.

The whispering grew louder.

'Silence,' Constantine ordered, that wind becoming a low, howling gale.

The whispering stopped.

The tension that had gathered in the room the moment Valentin had appeared pulled so tight it was nearly unbearable.

I forced my gaze away from Valentin to look at my fiancé instead, because I had the oddest feeling that Constantine wasn't so much shocked at his brother's appearance as he was angry.

Incandescently angry.

I wanted to say something, to stop whatever was going to happen next, because I knew it would be terrible; I just knew it. But I felt paralysed by shock, my throat too thick to force words through.

'You look perturbed,' Valentin observed casually, strolling closer to his brother. 'Understandable, what with me coming back like Lazarus, on top of managing this farce of a funeral. Well, don't worry, I won't take up too much more of your valuable time. I'll just take what's mine and then be on my way.' That intense black gaze of his flicked back to me and he held out a peremptory hand in my direction. 'Come, Olivia.'

I stared at him, my head full of memories.

Memories of the last time I'd seen him, on the small hidden beach, the one that no one else had known about; the one that had been our special place. It had been night, the black sky above scattered with jewel-bright stars, and he'd kissed me for the first time.

He'd whispered in the dark that one day, when we were both old enough and free of our families, we'd get married and be together for ever.

I'd never wanted anything so badly.

We'd lain in the sand, still warm from the day's heat, talking about how our life together would look and what we'd do. Marry, have a family, be free.

I'd loved him so much.

Then the next day he hadn't come down to the beach as he'd promised and it wasn't until later that I'd heard he and Constantine had been sent back to Madrid.

I'd never got to say goodbye. I'd been upset about it, but not worried. Because he'd had my mobile number and we could have texted each other and called.

Except he hadn't called. And he hadn't texted. And he hadn't emailed.

I'd never heard from him again.

Six months later, he was dead.

I'd only been fifteen and full of the desperate, dramatic emotions that often fill teenage girls. He'd been my first love, my first heartbreak.

But I was a woman now, not a child, and I'd left all of that behind me. I was stronger, harder and colder, as I'd needed to be to manage my company. So I had no idea why I was suddenly full of emotion, full of a blistering rage that left me shaking.

Because how dared he?

How dared he have left me without saying goodbye? Without a text, a call or even an email? How dared he break my heart like that, knowing how much I'd loved him? How dared he tell me he loved me, only to leave?

And, more than anything else, how dared he pretend to die?

I opened my mouth to tell him where he could stick his, 'Come, Olivia'.

Then all the lights went out and the ballroom was plunged into darkness.

For an instant, there was only silence.

Then the entire place erupted into chaos, people shouting and screaming.

I stayed where I was, rage and shock still coiling through me, making it difficult to think. Someone called my name, but I couldn't tell who it was or in what direction it had come from. Then I felt someone grab my hand, their grip large, warm and strong.

Constantine.

Strange that I should feel better with his hand holding mine, since I'd never needed reassurance from him before. Nevertheless, I did now, so I held tightly to him as he gently pulled me along through the blackness.

Light was coming through a doorway, his tall, broad figure momentarily blocking it out as he approached it. Behind me, I could still hear people shouting in confusion and the sound of smashing glass.

My heart was still beating far too fast, though my fear was receding.

What on earth had happened? Had there been a power failure or something? Yet, even as I thought it, I knew the idea was ludicrous.

The lights had gone out with perfect timing, just before Constantine had been about to take charge. Which meant it was no power failure.

Valentin had engineered it, I was sure, but why? To what end?

Constantine drew me through the doorway and I stood for a second, blinking as my eyes adjusted to the light. And, as they did, he turned around.

And my heart dropped all the way down into my uncomfortably high stilettos.

Because it wasn't Constantine.

It was Valentin.

CHAPTER TWO

Valentin

FINALLY. FINALLY, AFTER ALL those months of planning, Olivia Wintergreen was mine.

But then, she always had been.

Her clear, light-grey eyes had widened and I had been able to see the shock rippling over her pale, delicately featured face.

She'd assumed it was Constantine who'd taken her hand so naturally she'd be surprised to find it was me instead.

Her hand was cold, her fingers icy, and I remembered how she'd get cold after a swim in the sea, and I would take them in mine to warm them up. Once, I'd kissed the tips of her fingers and she'd laughed because it had tickled. She'd always had the most beautiful smile.

Except she wasn't smiling now.

Not that I expected her to.

I'd let her think I was dead—I'd let everyone

think I was dead—for the past fifteen years and so I hadn't exactly anticipated being welcomed with open arms.

She certainly wouldn't be happy when I got her back to my villa in the Maldives. But I'd deal with that later. Once she was there and safe, she'd have all the time in the world to yell at me.

First, though, I had to get her away from Constantine.

I'd planned this meticulously, right down to the very second I'd had my men cut the power, then I'd moved, crossing the space between us so it was my hand she'd grabbed in the darkness.

Me, leading her to safety.

I didn't have time for explanations, not with Constantine's security. I had to get her out of the mansion and with the least fuss possible before the confusion brought about by the power cut wore off and Constantine realised what had happened.

Yet even though I knew time was of the essence, for a second all I could do was stare at her, noting how changed she was.

She'd been fifteen the last time I'd seen her, all long, slender limbs and waist-length straight silver-blonde hair. A wildcat, yet with the sweetest smile I'd ever seen. My friend once, before she'd grown into something more.

She'd been so beautiful. The only thing I'd had in the hell of my childhood that had been mine.

Until Constantine had taken her from me.

Satisfaction was a cooling balm to the rage that had ignited inside me that moment six months ago when, during my daily press briefing, one of my staff had informed me that Constantine was now engaged to Olivia Wintergreen.

Well, he wouldn't be engaged to her much longer.

Just as he'd no longer be inheriting Silver Incorporated.

He might have had a couple of years' grace at being CEO if he hadn't involved Olivia. But he had. And now he would have to deal with the consequences.

The fury I'd glimpsed in Olivia's eyes just before I'd had the power killed leapt again, and she tried to jerk her hand away.

I tightened my grip. I didn't want her running, not before I had a chance to secure her. I'd been forced to give her up all those years ago and I wasn't going to let her be taken from me a second time.

'For God's sake, Valentin, what are you doing?' she demanded, those diamond-bright eyes of hers flashing. 'Let me go!'

Perhaps if I'd been kinder and more reassuring, gentler, things might have gone differently. But I wasn't. Because the boy who'd once had all those qualities was dead. He'd died in that car accident all those years ago.

And someone else had taken his place.

I wasn't Valentin Silvera any longer and I hadn't been for fifteen years.

I'd left him behind in the wreckage of that burned-out car, along with some of my DNA, in an effort to finally escape that bastard Domingo once and for all.

Now I was just Val, CEO of a company that had its roots in the shadier of Europe's crime networks, but was now straighter than an arrow, dealing with all kinds of security from tech to personnel to equipment.

And I wasn't kind or gentle or reassuring any longer.

I smiled at Olivia, my bright little star. 'Oh, sweetheart, I'm not letting you go. I'm not letting you go ever.'

Another woman might have been scared, but fear had never ruled Olivia before, and it didn't now.

Temper glittered in her eyes, her pale cheeks flushing pink.

Standing at Constantine's side, she'd been tall and slender as a lily, dressed in a plain yet expensively tailored dress of sombre black wool,

as was fitting for a funeral. The colour hadn't
suited her, making her look even paler and more
washed-out than she actually was, yet her expression had been diamond-hard.

She seemed so different from the young girl I
remembered. She'd been such a passionate little
thing back then, a ray of sunshine in the darkness of my childhood. I'd been drawn to her,
unable to help myself, at first fascinated by that
passion and then, as I'd got to know her, by the
sweet smile that she saved for me alone, the one
that reminded me of a summer dawn.

There were no smiles now, but I could still
see her passion in her anger, lighting her up
from the inside like someone had put a candle
inside her and lit the wick.

'You're insane.' Her chin lifted with all the
defiance and authority of an empress giving the
order for war. 'Let me go before Constantine
calls his security team.'

'He can try.' I tightened my grip and held
her fast, noting that her fingers no longer felt
so cold. 'But I've had my men infiltrating his
staff for the past six months so, unfortunately
for him, it is no longer "his" security team.'

Her gaze flickered. Was that fear I saw there?
I didn't want her to be afraid, but if she was it
couldn't be helped. There wasn't time to allay

any fears, not when they'd involve more than a few complicated explanations.

Besides, she should already know that the very last thing I'd do was hurt her.

'I see.' There was no fear in her voice, only a cold, flat tone that made her sound like Constantine. 'What do you want with me, then?'

Her long, pale blonde hair had been coiled in a chignon at the back of her head and locked in place by what looked like a million hairpins and several bottles of hairspray. I was half-convinced that if I touched her hair it would feel as hard as the diamonds her company sold.

I didn't have time for this conversation, not right now, yet I found myself answering all the same. 'You really have to ask that question? What do you think I want with you? You're marrying my brother, and I can't have that.'

'So, what? Instead of sending me an email, or maybe even picking up the phone, you decided to infiltrate Constantine's security and disrupt your father's funeral with some bizarre kidnapping scheme?'

I laughed. 'Well, when you put it like that, it does sound a trifle…bizarre. But I have my reasons. Besides, if I had sent an email, would you have called off your engagement?'

'No, of course not.' Impatiently, she tugged

at her hand again, trying to get free. 'Let me go, damn you.' It wasn't a plea. It was an order.

Sadly for her, I had no time for orders.

Even if I had sent her an email, Constantine would never have let her go. He was too much like Domingo, which was why I had no choice except to take not only the company but Olivia as well.

Domingo Silvera destroyed people, and so did Constantine.

I would not allow him to destroy her. This was about keeping her safe from him and I would go to any lengths to ensure that.

So I didn't let her go. Instead, I pulled her in closer to me, watching her face with its delicate, precise features.

She'd lost the openness she'd once given me, the emotional honesty that had been so precious. Her expression held nothing but icy calm, and there was a hard quality to her, a toughness that hadn't been there before that belied her delicate build and pretty china-shepherdess face.

What had happened to her in the years since we'd last seen each other? I'd always hoped she'd forget me, that once the news of my death got out she'd put me behind her and move on with her life.

Except I'd known the instant she'd seen me

come into the ballroom that my hopes had been in vain.

She'd gone dead white, frozen in shock like everyone else in the room, and for a brief second I'd regretted being so public with my plan.

But secrecy wouldn't have worked and would have given Constantine some measure of cover if he'd retaliated. Plus, the world needed to know I was back in order for me remove him as CEO of Silver Inc. So why not make a public gesture of it? And what better timing than at that bastard's funeral?

Olivia would get over the shock and, indeed, it looked as if she already had, her hard expression betraying absolutely nothing, not even a trace of the fury I'd seen before.

I could feel the resistance in her arm, but I didn't relent, bringing her in closer.

Where had that fury gone? Was it still there? Did it mean she still felt something for me after all these years? Perhaps she didn't. It had been a long time and we'd only been teenagers, after all.

Or perhaps she'd been angry because I was taking her away from Constantine. Did she love him? My research indicated that she didn't; I thought they hadn't slept together, but had she let him touch her after all?

I could feel my own jealous rage rise at the

thought, and I let it, since anger had always been a useful fuel for me.

Domingo had once told me that emotions were vulnerabilities and they had no place in his world; that I needed to free myself of them, because only then could I become the great man I was destined to be.

But he'd been wrong. He'd always been wrong.

Anger was power. Anger was fuel. And I burned it without compunction.

'Valentin,' she said coldly. 'I have my own security team. They're all military trained and, if you don't let me go right this second, they will end you.'

'Call them. They can try to end me, but I've died before and, as you can see, it didn't take.'

'If you don't—'

'You're not going anywhere except with me,' I said. 'So you might as well come willingly.'

'I will never come willingly, not with you.'

I shrugged. 'Then you will come unwillingly. The former will be easier for both of us; the latter will be inconvenient, but nothing more than that.'

Despite her icy expression, her breathing was fast and the pulse at the base of her throat was frantic. Again, though, she wasn't afraid; I could see that clearly. No; what she was, was furious.

Ah, that brought back memories…

I pulled her in even closer. So close I could hear her breath catch. Her perfume was faint and subtle, sophisticated. That was new; she hadn't worn perfume back when she was fifteen. Yet beneath that perfume I could smell something ineffably sweet, like honeysuckle. Her…

I remembered lying on warm sand beneath a star-studded sky, my own heart beating hard as I brushed my mouth over hers. Her lips had been soft, as velvety as rose petals, and she'd given the most delicious little sigh, as if she'd been waiting all her life for my kiss.

Now her eyes darkened as she stared up at me, like quartz filled with thunderclouds. Was she remembering that same moment? That same night? Did she remember that kiss as I did?

She looked delicate. As though she were made of spun glass.

A feeling tightened in my chest that wasn't anger, for a change, yet I didn't know what else it could be. And, though I wasn't gentle any more, I said, 'I won't harm you, little star. But you will come with me. I'm afraid you have no choice in the matter.'

For a second I thought she might give in, melt against me the way she had when we'd been young, giving me her trust and her surrender.

But she didn't.

Instead, she shook herself, giving me a look of the most complete disdain. 'I think not.'

And the feeling inside me twisted again, turning into something else.

Anticipation.

That girl she'd once been hadn't gone, it seemed. Under that diamond-hard veneer, little Olivia Wintergreen was still a wildcat.

Good. I liked a strong woman. And a strong woman who challenged me? Even better.

How had Constantine handled this new version of her? Had he tested that stubbornness? Had he broken through her diamond walls? Or did the pair of them freeze each other out?

Suddenly I was desperate to know, and know everything about their relationship. She would tell me. I'd make her. And then I'd make sure she never thought of him again.

Olivia opened her mouth, no doubt to tell me she'd scream again, but time was running out and I'd already lingered too long.

Before she could get a word out, I lifted her up and tossed her over my shoulder.

For a second she lay still, draped over me, her body warm as I turned in the direction of the front door. I thought I might get out without her creating a fuss.

Then she went stiff. 'Valentin! What the hell are you doing? Put me down!'

I smiled. There she was, the wild Olivia I remembered. 'What do you think?' I put an arm around her thighs to keep her steady and to stop her from kicking, which she probably would. 'I already told you that you were coming with me.'

'Don't you dare!' A fist thumped hard against my back. 'My security are armed!'

'Not any more, little star,' I said. 'My team have already secured their weapons. But feel free to scream on your way out.'

Then, gripping her tightly, I strode out of Constantine's mansion, Olivia Wintergreen screaming a furious blue streak all the way.

CHAPTER THREE

Olivia

THE MOST DELIGHTFUL warm breeze washed over me. It was gentle and brought with it the smell of salt and the heavy, sweet scent of tropical flowers.

I stretched, not wanting to open my eyes, because the bed I was lying in was so comfortable and the breeze felt good brushing over my bare skin…

Wait…

My *bare* skin? Since when had I slept in anything but pyjamas?

My eyes popped open, an unfamiliar ceiling above me.

Rafters in a honey-gold wood criss-crossed the big vaulted, empty space, a white fan turning lazily above the bed. Strange, silky-looking patterns of light rippled over the exposed ceiling, almost as if it was the reflection of the sun shining on water...

I stared at the patterns, not taking it in.

My brain felt sluggish, my head vaguely achy and my mouth dry, as if I'd had an emotional overload at some point, or a crying jag, which couldn't be right. Not when I liked to stay in control at all times. Had I somehow forgotten myself at Domingo's funeral and wake? I hadn't been grieving him, not when I hadn't liked him in the first place.

The wake... The shadow in the doorway...

My breath caught as memory came sliding in slowly like the tide.

Valentin.

A flush of violent heat went through me as the memories came flooding back. Valentin's sensational appearance... Constantine's fury... My own intense shock. And then the lights had gone out and someone had taken my hand in theirs, warm and reassuring. Except it hadn't been Constantine's hand, as I'd assumed, and I could still feel the shock as the tall man had turned round and I'd found Valentin's black gaze burning into mine.

'I'm never letting you go...'

The memories came flooding in even faster. He'd picked me up and slung me over his shoulder as if I weighed nothing, ignoring my shouts of rage and my fists hammering his strong back. He'd carried me out, tossed me into a car that had been waiting in the driveway and then, before I'd known what was happening, I was being driven away. He hadn't come with me and, not twenty minutes later, I'd found myself at private airfield being ushered into a sleek jet by two burly security staff.

Furious, I'd tried to argue with them—demanding an explanation, demanding to know where I was being taken, demanding to speak to Valentin—but all I'd got back was silence. I'd tried threats next, but that hadn't worked, either.

Valentin had arrived a few minutes later and proceeded directly past where I was sitting, heading to the work space at the back of the plane. He hadn't even looked at me.

Then we'd been in the air and, when I'd finally been able to unbuckle my seatbelt, I'd tried to confront him, only to be prevented from getting anywhere near him by the same stony-faced bodyguards.

I think at that point I might have shouted. I'd definitely called him every name under the sun and then some.

Then, left with nothing else to do, all my fury expended, I'd gone back to my seat and had promptly fallen asleep, exhausted.

Now I sat bolt-upright, looking round wildly

at the four-poster hung with gauzy white curtains that had been drawn back.

I was sitting in the middle of the vast mattress of that four-poster bed, a white sheet wrapped around me. The room was big, the walls panelled in that same honey-golden wood, the floors the same colour, and directly opposite me were huge sliding glass doors. The doors had been pulled back to admit a wonderful breeze and I saw immediately that in fact, the pattern on the ceiling *was* the reflection of the sunlight on water.

Through the doors was the ocean. A deep, intense turquoise-blue ocean.

A lagoon with a reef lay just beyond.

A wooden deck lay outside the doors and I could see stairs leading down from it, presumably straight into that beautiful water.

I didn't move, staring at the tropical sea a stone's throw from the bed, my heartbeat loud in my ears, along with the sound of water lapping gently against wood.

All I could see was Valentin's black eyes and all I could feel was his hand enveloping mine, the heat of his skin burning me, and his body as he'd drawn me in close, hard and hot. Not the body of a teenage boy any longer, but of a man. A broad-shouldered, powerful man.

He'd smelled so good, like cinnamon and cedar: warm and spicy and delicious...

'Feel free to scream on your way out...'

And just like that the rage of the night before returned. There was no trace of my cool, calm façade now. It had been crushed by the weight of the fury that washed through me.

Fury at being taken here against my will.

Fury at someone who was supposed to be dead, someone I'd loved and mourned, who was clearly not dead and had somehow duped everyone into thinking he was.

Fury at myself for being so weak and allowing all of that to happen.

And, just as I was fulminating about that, another thought struck me.

I looked down, pulling up the sheet wrapped around me.

Yes, as I'd suspected: I wasn't wearing the black dress I'd put on for the funeral. I'd been put into a delicate nightgown of white silk instead.

I was supposed to be focused and driven and in command of my emotions. I wasn't supposed to let them command me.

My father had always been very clear about that. He'd wanted a son to inherit his company but, as my mother had been unable to have any more children after me, he hadn't been able to

have one. So he'd done his best to mould me
into his idea of the perfect CEO, despite my
being female. And the perfect CEO was ambitious and cold and above all strong.

I wanted to be all those things. I didn't want
to be like my trophy-wife mother, fluttering
around ineffectually, all weepy and emotional,
doing everything my father told her in a futile
effort to make up for the sin of not producing
a son. He had been a difficult man, and my
mother had never stood up to him. She'd let
him walk all over her, and one thing I'd sworn
to myself was that I'd never let any man do that
to me. I'd never stay with a man who treated me
that way. I'd never be her.

So, I wasn't. I cultivated my ambition and
kept my emotions locked away in a box. I was
strong and in control.

But in that moment I forgot every single
lesson my father had drilled into me as fury
gripped me, hot and bright and intense. I
launched myself off the bed, clutching the sheet
around me.

I was going to find Valentin Silvera and then
I was going to wring his neck.

With my bare hands.

And then movement caught my eye from the
deck outside beyond the big, glass sliding doors.

A man was coming up the stairs from the ocean.

He was still wet, the sheen of water on his bare, deeply tanned skin glistening in the sun highlighting the width of powerful shoulders, the planes of a broad chest, the carved corrugations of his rock-hard stomach and the length of his strong thighs.

Water dripped from his night-black hair and, as he reached the deck, he shoved one long-fingered hand through it, pushing it back from his face.

I froze in the middle of the bedroom, my fury forgotten for an instant.

He was stunningly beautiful.

He was also very, very naked.

Blood rushed into my cheeks.

It was, of course, Valentin.

'Good morning, little star,' he said as if he wasn't entirely naked, his voice deep, rich and much warmer than Constantine's had ever been. 'I see you're awake.'

My cheeks were burning, shivers of heat whispering over my skin. I wanted to look away from him and yet at the same time I wanted to keep staring, mesmerised at the sight of all that masculine glory.

He'd always been tall back when we were children, and in the water of that hidden beach I'd given him covert glances. At thirteen I'd been strangely compelled and at the same time oddly flustered by how muscular his body was.

He'd been beautiful then, and he was beautiful now, and I was very conscious that I was not thirteen any longer.

I'd steered clear of men altogether after Valentin had supposedly died, and since I'd taken over the company they'd steered clear of me. I'd been told I was too intimidating, which had been pleasing, and not something I wanted to change.

I'd never met anyone I'd wanted to change for, anyway. And I still hadn't.

Except this feeling now...wanting to look at him, touch him, see if his skin was as velvety and hot as it looked, glistening and brown in the heat of a tropical sun... It was unfamiliar sexual attraction and I didn't like it.

Part of the reason I'd decided to marry Constantine was because, though I admired his cold beauty, I didn't feel any need to touch it. I wasn't attracted to him, no matter that he looked like Valentin, which was exactly what I'd wanted.

Having children together would require some amount of touching, but I deliberately hadn't thought about that aspect of it. It was the child I'd get at the end that mattered to me. I didn't think about sex, full-stop.

'Something the matter?' Valentin drawled,

straightening up to his full height, his beautiful mouth curving in a wicked smile that sent yet more prickles of heat scattering all over my skin. 'Or did you see something you liked?'

My fury returned no matter how hard I tried to ignore it, doubling at my reaction to his nakedness.

It shouldn't bother me. I should have been over him years ago. I'd cried for him so many times and then, on the first anniversary of his death, my father had told me to snap out of it; that he was gone and all the crying in the world wouldn't bring him back. I should divert my energies into my school work, because didn't I want to go to university? Didn't I want to take over the company?

So, I'd told myself to stop being so stupid. Valentin was gone, and he'd dumped me anyway, so why was I crying for a boy who'd made me all those empty promises and then never spoke to me again?

My father had been right—crying was weak and pointless and it wouldn't bring Valentin back—so I'd stopped and had never cried over him again.

'I want answers.' I ignored his comment as I clutched my sheet around me. 'And you will give them to me. Now.'

'Oh, I will, will I?' His smile was all flame,

hot and wicked, flickering around his mouth. 'And what will you give me if I do? I can think of several things already.'

'I'm not giving you anything,' I snapped, struggling despite myself to keep my gaze firmly on his face. 'You owe me, Valentin. A few answers is the very least you can give me.'

'I owe you, hmm?'

I took a step towards him, unable to help myself, my fury raging at the leash I was trying to keep on it. 'You kidnapped me, you bastard. And then undressed me.'

'Yes, so I did. Sorry about that.' He did not sound the slightest bit sorry. 'You'd fallen asleep, so I carried you off the plane then had a staff member put you in that nightgown, because who wants to be in the same clothes for fifteen hours straight? And, as for the kidnapping, well…it was the quickest and easiest way to get you out of Madrid.'

None of that mollified me in any way.

'I didn't want to leave Madrid.' I took another step. 'Where am I? What am I doing here? Why did you bring me here? And what happened to you?' The words spilled out of me heedlessly and I had to lock my jaw to stop myself from saying any more.

From telling him how you cried for him and how he broke your heart.

No, God, no. I never wanted him to know that. I'd spent years armouring myself against that kind of pain and I would never again willingly open myself up the way I had back when I was fifteen.

I was Olivia Wintergreen, CEO of Wintergreen Fine Diamonds. My father had always told me that in order to manage the company you had to be a diamond. You had to be hard, bright and sharp. Flawless in every way.

And so a diamond I'd become.

Valentin said nothing for a long moment, his hot gaze roaming over me, his expression giving absolutely nothing away.

Then, before I could move or make a sound, he strode towards me, still dripping wet and scattering water droplets. Two steps and he was in front of me, his hot gaze on mine.

'Did you miss me, Livvy?' He reached out, his fingertips brushing my cheekbone, his touch bypassing all my armour, scorching right down to the centre of my soul. 'It's been such a long time. Too long.'

He was so close, the spicy scent of his skin half-drowned by the fresh salt of the ocean he'd just been swimming in, and I was instantly transported back to that night on the hidden beach.

It had been one of those warm, tropical nights

when the air had been heavy with the smell of flowers and yet cool enough to be pleasant. We'd just been swimming, even though my father had forbidden me to go swimming in the sea at night. He wouldn't have been happy with me being with Valentin, either—if he'd known.

I'd loved Val so much. I hadn't wanted to be with anyone else.

Our skin had been damp from our swim and we'd lain in the sand together. My whole body had felt alive with awareness of him so close to me. And then he'd raised himself up on one elbow and looked down at me, reached out and brushed his fingertips across my cheek, as he'd done just now…

I'd trembled, wanting him to kiss me so badly.

And he had. Lowering his head, his mouth on mine so unexpectedly soft, and warm…

I shoved the memories away. Hard.

'What's going on, Valentin?' I demanded, forcing the husky sound from my voice. 'Why am I here? I have to get back to Madrid.'

'You're not going back to Madrid.' He didn't smile this time, his hand dropping away. 'You're not marrying him, Olivia. I forbid it.'

'What do you mean, you forbid it?' I stared at him in outrage as he turned away, going back out onto the deck to grab the white towel from the sun-lounger.

'You heard me.' He dried himself off with brisk strokes, then casually draped the towel around his neck, gripping the ends in his large, long-fingered hands, still making no effort whatsoever to hide his nakedness. 'You can't marry him. I won't let you.'

'You…won't *let* me?' For a minute all I could do was blink in astonishment at his arrogance, his sheer audacity. 'As I recall, no one died and made you king.'

Amusement glittered in his eyes. 'There's still time.'

There was an edge to him I could see. An edge that hadn't been there before, or maybe I'd just never noticed, but one thing was for sure: that edge was razor-sharp.

I took a breath. This wasn't the boy I'd known. This was someone different, a harder man, a man infinitely more dangerous than the boy had ever been.

He's fascinating…

The thought crossed my mind and instantly I pushed it away. No, I definitely wasn't going there. No matter that my heart was a guarded fortress these days and men were of no interest to me at all; he'd kidnapped me and dragged me halfway across the world without asking, and all because he didn't want me to marry his brother.

He was mad and there was nothing fascinating about that.

'I'm going to the police,' I said coldly. 'And when I tell them—'

'You're not a prisoner, Olivia,' Valentin interrupted. 'You may leave whenever you want.'

'But you just said—'

'Admittedly you'll have to fly yourself home, since I only have one pilot and he's not here. But you're welcome to try it.'

The fury inside me leapt again and I moved, striding past him, still clutching my sheet, stepping onto the deck outside the bedroom and into the dense tropical heat.

The deck seemed to wrap around the entire house so I kept on walking, determined to figure out where I was and how I could get away.

I was right about the deck, it did wrap around the entire house, which was built over the clear, turquoise-blue water. A tiny island, a jewel-bright stud of green with crystalline white sand surrounding it, lay behind the house. The deck led onto a jetty that stretched from the island right into the deeper waters of the lagoon.

But there was nothing tied up at the end of the jetty. No boats. No planes. And there was nothing in the sea, just endless blue water, the sun striking sparks from the surface, the scented air warm and humid.

I was breathing hard, sweating in the heat, an anger I couldn't fight burning in my chest like a hot coal.

He'd lied. I *was* a prisoner. There was no way off this tiny island and he knew it.

I turned back to the house, though 'house' was too simple a word for the sprawling, luxury villa built over the water that looked like it was hanging suspended over the lagoon.

It had been a long time since I'd been to the tropics. I didn't like the sun or the heat, or the sand that seemed to get everywhere; not these days. I burned easily and I loathed having to constantly put on sunscreen and wear a hat to stop from getting sunburned.

I didn't want to be here.

I wanted to be back in Madrid. Or, no, what I actually wanted was to be back in London, in the gracious old home in Hampstead where my mother still lived. Back where everything was familiar and I was in control of things.

A thought flashed through my head.

What about Wintergreen? What about the debts? What about the board? What would they do when they discovered I'd been kidnapped by Valentin?

And Constantine? What about him?

My stomach lurched. Constantine… He'd known Valentin and I had been more than friends when we were teenagers, but he'd never mentioned it to me, not once. He'd never even spoken his brother's name. Would he come searching for me? Or would he think I'd gone with Valentin willingly? And, if he did, would he still want to marry me?

You'd better hope so otherwise you can say goodbye to Wintergreen.

The hot coal in the centre of my chest burned hotter, brighter. Those debts needed paying and the board had been looking for a way to get rid of me ever since Dad had died. They didn't like the fact that I was a woman and they liked the changes I wanted to institute even less. This would give them the perfect excuse to let me go.

Damn Valentin. Damn him to hell.

I had to get back. I *had* to. I'd worked too hard to get where I was, to prove I could manage the family company better than any son, and I couldn't let that slip through my fingers just because of some idiot man.

I strode back along the deck, the wood smooth and warm beneath my bare feet, the sheet still wrapped around me fluttering in the warm breeze.

Valentin had come out to stand on the deck outside the bedroom.

Mercifully he'd pulled on some clothes—a simple white T-shirt and worn jeans—and now he stood there, impossibly tall, impossibly gorgeous, his hands in his pockets, watching me.

His posture was casual, but the smile on his face was the fierce, predator's smile he'd been wearing when he'd appeared at the wake.

A panther who'd captured his prey and was now contemplating exactly the best way to eat it.

Except I wasn't prey.

'There, you see?' he said as I strode back to him. 'You can go wherever you want.'

But I didn't stop.

It felt as if I'd always had this anger burning inside me, an anger I'd had to swallow for the last fifteen years in order to prove myself worthy enough to manage Wintergreen, even though I'd had the misfortune of being born female.

'They'll never respect you if come over too emotional,' Dad had used to tell me about the board when he'd finally had to accept that, if he wanted the family company to remain in family hands, he was going to have to leave it to me. 'If you want them on your side, you have to be confident. You have to be cold.

'Be a diamond,' he'd gone on. 'Diamonds are beautiful, but they're also hard and sharp. They're created under pressure, so they're strong. And that's how you will be too.'

And so that was how I was.

But it turned out that, right now, I was not a diamond.

Instead of being hard and sharp and cold, I was seething with frustrated fury. At Valentin for upending my carefully ordered life and putting my company at risk. Not to mention tumbling me back into all the emotional chaos I thought I'd put behind me.

I raised my hand and slapped him hard across the face.

CHAPTER FOUR

Valentin

SHE WAS MAGNIFICENT striding towards me, her hair tossed by the breeze and trailing out behind her like a veil, the sheet moulding to her curves and outlining perfect round breasts, the swell of her hips and slender thighs…

She was perfection, a vengeful goddess with her silver eyes flashing and her cheeks glowing pink.

There was no sign of her hard veneer, not now. No, there was nothing but the white-hot passion that had always lived inside her, that used to make her burn like a star.

And she was burning now.

Desire gripped me, intense and hungry. I'd always used to wonder what she'd be like as a woman, and I'd thought I'd get to see her become that woman too, if it hadn't been for Constantine. Now here she was in all her glory…

I wanted her. And, since I denied myself nothing, I would have her.

However, since she was clearly going to slap me, perhaps I'd wait to broach the topic.

Sure enough, her hand came up and for a split second I debated grabbing her wrist before she could land a blow. But, if slapping me helped her feel better about the situation, then I'd let her.

Violence was certainly a choice but there were other, far more pleasant ways to get rid of excess emotion. Perhaps I could show her that once she realised hitting me wouldn't change anything.

So I didn't move and I didn't flinch as her blow landed. I'd had worse, much, *much* worse, though she wasn't to know that.

The crack of her palm against my cheekbone resounded in the humid air and it stung—she was surprisingly strong. I smiled. Pain could make pleasure that much more acute and I wasn't averse to it.

'Feel better?' I asked mildly.

She was breathing very fast, her pretty eyes darkened with fury. Then the anger began to recede and a look of shock crossed her face.

'Oh, my God,' she whispered as if to herself. 'What are you doing to me?'

But I didn't want that fire inside her dying,

didn't want that diamond veneer back in place, and as she started to back away I reached out and grabbed her wrist, pulling her closer to me. 'I didn't do anything,' I said. 'You did that all by yourself. And it was magnificent. You can even do it again, if you like. I don't mind. I enjoyed it.'

Her eyes were wide as they stared into mine and I could feel the tension between us grow then pull taut. Her skin was still pink and flushed, making her irises look darker, like charcoal instead of quicksilver, and the sun in her hair turned it into a deeper gold.

The sweet scent of her surrounded me, mingling with the salt to remind me of that secret Caribbean beach, situated between our respective holiday estates, where we used to meet. Of swimming, lying in the sand and talking about everything and nothing. Of driftwood fires and toasted marshmallows and arguments and apologies.

Of friendship that had grown slowly over time into something more…

She'd only been fifteen, and there had just been a kiss between us, but she'd had my heart even then. Just as she still had it.

And she's not fifteen now.

Her wrist in my hand felt delicate and fragile,

my fingers mapping the beat of her pulse. Her skin was warm and I could hear her breath catch.

For a second, I thought she might lean forward and press those petal-soft lips against mine.

I could almost taste her kiss…

She ripped her wrist from my grip and took a couple of steps back, shaking her head. Then she turned around, her back to me, her spine stiff and ramrod-straight, looking out over the endless blue of the Indian Ocean.

I could feel the blood pumping hot in my veins, the sound of my own heartbeat loud in my head. I'd been certain for a moment there that she was going to soften for me, kiss me, let out that passion I knew lived inside her. But apparently not.

It made me want to close the distance between us very badly, to pull her into my arms, shatter that hard veneer of hers and discover the sweetness of her kiss once again. To tug away the sheet and bear her pale skin. Then pull her down onto that sun-lounger and have her right here beneath the sun.

I could. Even though she'd pulled away from me, I'd seen the flicker of desire in her eyes. It hadn't been all anger. She wanted me, I knew it; and, if I kissed her, she'd melt against me the way she'd done all those years ago.

Is that really how you want it to happen?

I stared at the tense line of her shoulders. Her whole posture was tight.

No, I'd never denied myself anything I wanted. Nothing at all. And that included all the forbidden emotions my father had despised: anger, love, lust, guilt, hate, grief…

But nothing was forbidden to me now. Anger in particular I enjoyed, because it gave everything such spice. Particularly sex.

Angry sex with Olivia would be incredible; I knew that. But something stopped me from closing that distance, from taking her the way I wanted to. I hated boundaries, hated rules. I loathed being restrained. Yet I stayed where I was, struggling with the unfamiliar urge to hold back.

I wasn't sure why, since I'd never held back before, but some long-forgotten instinct told me it was too soon to take her to bed.

I had a plan and I needed to stick to it. I was to get her here and keep her here until I'd neutralised Constantine as a threat. Then I'd rebuild the relationship we'd once had, make her fall in love with me once again and marry me.

So she'd be mine, and only mine, for ever.

I could certainly manipulate her into bed. It wouldn't be the first time I'd manipulated someone to get what I wanted, after all; that was exactly how I'd built my business. But it wouldn't be quite as satisfying as her climbing into my bed because she wanted me. Because she was desperate for me.

Desperate for me the way she had been all those years ago.

You were desperate too, don't forget.

Oh, yes, I was. I'd had all kinds of plans for how we could be together, away from my father and out of his reach for ever. Away from the beatings, the lessons and the tests. Away from his attempts to turn Constantine and me into his mirror image.

Cold. Hard. And above all, strong.

I had never passed his tests. Never learned his lessons. I'd never followed his rules and he'd punished me for it. Repeatedly.

Constantine, on the other hand, had done whatever Domingo had asked him to do. He had been Domingo's ideal son, learning all the lessons Domingo beat into us, becoming cold and hard, becoming Domingo himself.

So much so that when Domingo had told me I had to give Olivia up and I'd refused, continuing to meet her in secret, Constantine had told him exactly what I was doing.

My brother used to spy on us down on our hidden beach and she'd met him a couple of times. Once or twice I'd suspected he wanted

Olivia for himself, but he was too cold a fish for her, and she'd preferred me. Then he'd told Domingo that I was still meeting with her and I knew then it wasn't her he wanted.

It was Domingo he'd thrown his lot in with.

And whose fault was that?

It was mine, of course. I'd failed to protect him from Domingo's manipulations and, in the end, he'd turned against me. He'd become Domingo, and I took full responsibility. That was why it was up to me to save the company and all the people in it from him, and to save Olivia too.

No one else knew that Domingo had been a psychopath, and that Constantine had become just like him.

No one except me.

So, no, I wouldn't manipulate her. That was something Domingo would have done, and I'd never stoop to that. But patience I was good at, patience I could do, and so I'd wait for her to come to me.

'I have a few tasks I need to complete,' I said to her slender back. 'And they're likely to take most of the day. However, we'll meet tonight for dinner and I'll answer your questions then.'

She didn't turn. 'And my company? What about that? What about my fiancé?'

Fiancé? No. He is not *her fiancé any longer.*

The thought of my brother brought my anger back to the boil and I let it bubble there for a moment, giving it some time.

Then I killed the heat, just because I could.

'You are free to explore the villa and the island,' I replied. 'Nothing is off-limits. There is clothing you can change into in the bedroom and I'll have a laptop brought to you in case you wish to work.'

Her head turned sharply at that, giving me her exquisite profile. 'Work?'

'Well, you did ask about your company. It's… at a delicate stage, I understand.' And it was. I'd seen all the financials, since I had my ways of finding out information, especially information other people didn't want known.

Olivia glanced at me over her shoulder, her expression utterly unreadable. 'What makes you say that?'

I debated revealing the full extent of my knowledge of her and everything she'd done since she'd been eighteen years old. Would it help my cause? Or would she find it creepy? Probably the latter.

Then again, I made no apology for it. Someone had to protect her and, while Domingo had been alive, that someone was always going to be me.

'Oh, I know all about you, little star,' I said

gently. 'Everything. From how your father left Wintergreen on the brink of collapse due to some terrible investments, to how much Constantine is going to pay to prop it up. I know all about the degrees you worked so hard to earn and how you came top of your class in all of them. I know that you have few friends and that you've never once had a boyfriend. And I know that you're lonely and that, while Constantine will save your company, he'll kill all of your passion stone-dead.'

She went very still, as if she'd been frozen. An ice statue of a woman.

'I've been watching you,' I went on. 'Since you were eighteen years old. You needed protection and the only person who could give that was me.'

She said nothing for a long moment before turning around fully to face me.

I'd always been able to read her expressions; she'd never hidden how she felt from me. But now… I had no idea what she was thinking.

'Protect me?' She raised one imperious brow. 'Protect me from what?'

I'd hooked her; I could see that. She wanted to know more.

Which was my cue to leave.

'If you want to know, meet me tonight for

dinner.' I smiled. 'I told you I'd answer your questions then and I meant it.'

I didn't wait for her to reply; I just turned around and went back inside.

Before I gave all my secrets away.

CHAPTER FIVE

Olivia

IMMEDIATELY I TRIED to find a way off the island.

I didn't bother to dress, striding down the deck to the island itself still wrapped in my sheet.

There were a couple of staff members I tried to talk to, but they either didn't speak English or didn't want anything to do with me, because they shook their heads and walked away before I could get a word out.

It was frustrating.

The island itself was small and covered with palms and some kind of dense, scrubby trees that made exploring off the pretty white shell paths that wound along the shore next to impossible. Not that I wanted to go charging around in the undergrowth wrapped only in a sheet and a nightgown anyway.

What was very clear, though, was that there

were no handy boat sheds hiding boats I could climb into and use to sail away. In the end I had to accept that I was trapped on the island, with no way off it, and wandering around in a sheet wasn't going to get me anywhere, nor was being inarticulately furious about it.

Eventually, I went back to the villa in search of clothes. In the bedroom there was a wide built-in wardrobe with sliding mirrored doors, and inside were a lot of built-in drawers and shelves. There were rails too, with the prettiest dresses and skirts and long shirts hanging up, all floaty and light and made for wafting about in.

I preferred sharp business suits and tailoring, armour that helped the board of Wintergreen remember who I was—not a mere woman, but Wintergreen's CEO, and a better leader than my father ever had been.

Except there were no sharps suits and tailoring in this wardrobe, only pretty, floaty things that reminded me far too much of my mother, who was always pretty and feminine because that was how my father had liked her to be.

She'd done whatever he'd wanted, constantly trying to make up for having had me instead of the son he'd always longed for, and then for not being able to have any more children.

She'd blamed herself for that and had always

been apologising to him for it. She'd loved him. That had been the problem. And, because she'd loved him, she'd stayed with him, even though he hadn't respected her and hadn't even seemed to like her.

I've never been able to understand why she'd stayed.

Love, that was the problem. Love turned you into a door mat and I didn't want anything to do with it.

I had no choice about the clothes, though. If I didn't want to trail around wearing a sheet all day, I was going to have to wear something hanging on those rails.

First, though, I had a shower in the huge white-tiled *en suite* bathroom, with a bath standing in the middle of the room directly in front of a huge window that looked out over the pristine lagoon.

There was something about the views of the lagoon and the reef, the clear, brilliant turquoise of the water and whiteness of the sand, that tugged at my soul. It reminded me of places I didn't want to remember and feelings I thought I'd buried.

It was disturbing, so I ignored them as I showered and then walked back into the bedroom, going over to the wardrobe to choose something to wear. There appeared to be no underwear, which was annoying, since I'd been wearing mine for a while now and I wanted something clean. There were only bikinis, so I put on a pretty lavender one with string ties at the hip. It wasn't something I'd ever choose to wear myself, but, if I thought about it as a bra and a pair of knickers, then that was okay.

Briefly, I wondered why Valentin had a wardrobe full of women's clothing then decided it was probably better not to wonder. Whatever the reason, I didn't want to know.

There was a lovely light-blue dress that I grabbed to wear over the top of the bikini with a V-necked empire line and long, floaty silk skirts, and it seemed to fit well. It wasn't my thing at all, and the feeling of the silk brushing over my bare skin made me uncomfortably aware of my own virtual nakedness beneath it, but there wasn't anything else to wear. And at least it was cool.

Dressed, I went to explore the villa.

It was large and sprawling, panelled in that honey-gold wood, with simple furniture upholstered in white linen. Folk art sculptures had been placed on low tables and there were simple yet effective abstracts on the walls.

Everything about it was low key, mainly because the view of the lagoon—which could be seen from every room—was so spectacular nothing could compete with it.

The only sound was the ocean lapping against the supports of the villa, the sounds of sea birds and, every so often, the drone of a far-off boat or plane.

It was beautiful. Peaceful. And a part of me wanted to lie down on one of the long, low couches with a book and curl up to read. Or throw off the silky dress and dive into the warm, inviting water.

But I couldn't. This wasn't a holiday. I'd been kidnapped and brought here by Valentin and I needed to figure out what was going on back home and how I could possibly fix it.

I couldn't afford the Wintergreen board to think of me as a damsel in distress, which meant getting in touch with my management team to let them know where I was and try to instigate some kind of damage control.

I also needed to get in touch with Constantine and let him know I was okay.

In the main living area, on a low table, a phone and a laptop had been laid out and, since it was clear they were for my use, I went to them immediately.

I couldn't get hold of Constantine so I left him a voicemail. Then I called Rachel, my PA, and the first thing she said was, 'Why are you calling me when you're supposed to be on holiday?'

'Holiday?' I echoed, staring out through the big glass doors at the view of the lagoon. 'What holiday?'

'You took leave, remember? I've been telling you that for ages, and just last week you took a month's leave.'

I hadn't taken a month's leave. In fact, there was no way I would have, not with the company being at such a delicate stage, so why on earth did Rachel think that?

'Are you sure?' I asked. 'I don't recall…'

'Mr Silvera called a couple of days ago while you were in Madrid. He said he was planning to whisk you away for a special holiday.'

'Mr Silvera called you,' I repeated blankly, a sudden suspicion nagging at me.

'Yes. He sounded quite pleased about it.' Rachel gave a little sigh. 'So, come on, spill. Where did he take you? He said he wanted to surprise you.'

I gritted my teeth, the suspicion nagging even more insistently. 'Tell me, Rachel. Has anything…happened in the world recently? No kidnappings or abductions?'

'Kidnappings?' Rachel sounded surprised. 'I mean, probably somewhere. But there haven't been any in the news recently. Why?'

Mr Silvera had called my PA about a surprise holiday. And there had been no reports of kidnappings…

Constantine wouldn't take me away on a surprise holiday. He didn't do surprises in any shape or form, still less holidays. And as for the lack of reports of kidnappings…

Apparently, Constantine hadn't reported my abrupt abduction by the twin brother famously back from the dead. Why not?

'Thanks, Rachel,' I said shortly and disconnected the call, my heart beating fast.

I opened the laptop and turned it on, bringing up a web browser and doing a quick search of all the news websites.

There was nothing there about the return of Valentin Silvera. Nothing about how Olivia Wintergreen had been kidnapped from the wake for her late father-in-law-to-be. Nothing about any security incident at Constantine's Madrid mansion.

My heart thumped harder as I closed the laptop and stared at it.

It was Valentin who'd called Rachel, wasn't it? Valentin who'd pretended to be his brother, telling Rachel I was going on leave. And then, for some inexplicable reason, Constantine had somehow managed to keep his brother's sudden reappearance and my kidnapping out of the media.

Why? What were his intentions? Did he not want to find me? Did he not care? What on earth was going on?

I picked up the phone and rang my home number.

My mother picked up. 'Oh,' she said when she heard my voice, 'it's you. How is your holiday?'

So Valentin had called her too, pretending to be Constantine, letting her know that he was taking me away for a surprise holiday.

Perhaps I should have been grateful that he'd contacted people to let them know what was happening, but I wasn't.

The bastard had planned this down to the nth degree, hadn't he?

'I know everything about you, little star... Everything.'

My mother was blithely unaware of my distraction, even being the one to disconnect the call so I could get back to 'being with my fiancé'. He was a special man, she told me. I had to remember to pay him lots of attention.

But then, that was my mother. As long as the men were being paid lots of attention, everything was great.

After I'd finished speaking to her, I sat on the

comfortable couch, staring out over the lagoon, Valentin's words ringing in my head.

My palm stung as I remembered the crack of it across his cheek.

I'd been so angry. And beneath it, there had also been a healthy dose of confusion and shock. I'd been tumbled right back into the emotional chaos of that year when I'd fallen in love. When I'd been kissed then betrayed, and then suffered the most heart-breaking loss.

I'd been rebelling against Dad that year. He'd forbidden me from spending time with 'those Silvera boys', but I'd ignored him, sneaking off to the secret beach anyway, pouring out my anger to Valentin at his constant nit-picking at what he'd termed my 'ridiculous female tantrums', telling Val that I never wanted to run that stupid company, that he couldn't tell me what to do. I wanted to do what *I* wanted, not what he wanted.

But he had been right, my father. I *had* only been fifteen. And, after I'd lost Valentin, all the light had gone out of the world. It had become a darker, colder place, and so I'd become a darker, colder person.

I'd put aside my grief, my silly broken heart and my childish dreams. And I'd let the pressure turn me into a diamond, because nothing could touch a diamond.

Yet somehow, Valentin's shock return had touched me all the same. And the feelings I thought I'd excised from my heart had all returned with him.

I didn't want to feel that way again. It had never been part of my plan. What I wanted was to run the company, shake up all those stuffy traditionalists who thought me being a woman was a disadvantage and prove my father wrong.

He hadn't needed a son. He'd only needed me.

And it was a good thing that I was a woman, since marrying Constantine would pay off the debts my father had run up. The trade-off was having him take over for a year or two, just until the company got back on its feet again. It wasn't ideal, having a man taking over running the place for me, but that had been his price for his financial help, and I was prepared to pay it. He was also going to give me children and I wanted that as well.

IVF had been a possibility, but the process was time-consuming and gruelling physically, and if I had a man on call then why not use him?

Really, marrying Constantine had been the perfect solution to my problems.

Until Valentin had come along and upended my entire life.

My palm kept on stinging and I could still

see the flames in his black eyes and his edgy predator's smile. He'd let me hit him. He hadn't flinched. In fact, he'd even told me to hit him again. And then he'd wrapped his fingers around my wrist and pulled me close, so that all I could see were those black flames; all I was aware of was the intense heat of his body, his warm, spicy scent and the sensual shape of his mouth.

I'd remembered then our first kiss. How warm that mouth had been and how surprisingly soft. How it had felt on mine, sending shivers all over my skin.

That kiss had been magical.

That kiss had changed my life.

You want to kiss him again.

My fingers closed into a fist and I dug my nails savagely into my palm to get rid of that stinging sensation.

No, there would be no more kisses with Valentin. I'd said goodbye to the boy he'd once been and wasn't interested in the man he now was.

He'd kidnapped me and brought me halfway around the world, and it was clear he was intending to keep me here to 'protect me', whatever that meant.

And the only thing I was interested in was the answers he'd give me, because that was what

I was going to get from him tonight at dinner. He *would* tell me everything. And then I'd force him to take me home.

By any means necessary.

CHAPTER SIX

Valentin

THAT NIGHT, I MADE sure everything was perfect.

I had my staff arrange for a table covered with a white tablecloth to be placed on the end of the jetty. There was silver cutlery, the finest porcelain and the most delicate crystal glasses. Hurricane lamps were lit and placed at strategic points along the jetty, as well as around the table itself. The light was flickering and subtle, enough so we could see to eat, but not enough to obscure the stars.

I wanted there to be stars.

I'd also given the few house staff on the island the next two weeks off with double pay, as long as they went back to their homes on the other islands.

I wanted no interruptions. I wanted to be alone with Olivia for the next week, or even two, which hopefully would be plenty of time to bring her round to my way of thinking.

I'd spent most of the day catching up with my staff back in Europe, keeping tabs on Constantine and his reaction to my intention to remove him from his company, not to mention stealing away his bride-to-be.

My lawyers informed me that no one could get hold of him, that he'd disappeared, which was odd. Then, when I couldn't find any mention of my triumphant return from the dead on the web, I realised that somehow he'd managed to keep what had happened out of the media. Indeed, when I finally heard from my mole in Silver Inc, I learned that Constantine had given very specific instructions that no one was to talk about me or what had happened at Domingo's wake on pain of instant dismissal.

There was no mention of Olivia anywhere.

I was amused, mainly because I'd predicted that this would be Constantine's reaction. He wouldn't want anyone to know his twin was back from the dead, not until he'd figured out how to keep control of Silver Inc and block me from claiming it.

He was nothing if not relentless at holding on to what he wanted. He would hate that I had taken Olivia too, and no doubt he was already planning how to get her back.

I had a couple of security launches patrolling the seas around my island, though, plus a few insiders with the authorities on Male, the Maldives' biggest island. If Constantine tried to come for me here, I'd know about it within minutes.

However, it had already been twenty-four hours and he hadn't made a move; I couldn't deny I was curious as to why. Olivia wasn't the only person I'd watched. I'd watched Constantine too, and I knew that he felt nothing for her personally. He didn't feel anything for anyone. But she was important to him nonetheless, and I suspected that was simply because he'd been intending to make her his.

However, now I'd stolen her back, I was sure he wouldn't let that stand.

I sure as hell wouldn't have.

I left warnings with my security team to stay sharp and then, as the day slid into evening and the last of my staff set out dinner on the end of the jetty, I went down to supervise.

All Olivia's favourite foods were present and accounted for, as was her favourite drink as an adult—expensive French champagne. I wanted to show her that I still remembered what food she liked, and that I hadn't forgotten what we'd once been to each other.

Once all was ready, and my staff safely dispatched to their homes, I pulled out a chair and sat.

And waited for Olivia.

I hadn't specified a particular time for dinner, but she'd be able to see me, since the end of the jetty was visible from most rooms of the villa.

I wondered if she'd keep me waiting and was curious to see if she would. I would, if I were her, particularly if I was feeling petty.

Yet I hadn't been sitting there long before I watched her tall, slender figure coming down the jetty towards me.

A typical tropical sunset was staining the blue of the sky with reds and golds and pinks. The heat of the day had faded, leaving the air warm and pleasant and still.

A perfect evening.

Yet the woman coming towards me was more perfect still.

Her hair was loose and floating free down her back in a silver-gold fall, the sunset tingeing it pink and red, as it did her pale skin. She must have investigated the wardrobe in the bedroom, the one I'd stocked with pretty things for her to wear, because she had on one of my favourites—a dress of pale blue silk that clung to and flowed with the shape of her figure as she walked. The silk was so fine it was transparent and, rather disappointingly, she must also have found one of the bikinis and decided to wear that in lieu of underwear.

Well, eventually she wouldn't bother with a bikini. I'd make sure of that.

I stood as she came closer, because a gentleman should always stand when a lady approaches. Not that I was in any way a gentleman, but it was important to observe the niceties. Especially at so delicate a stage in the proceedings.

I didn't wait for her to say anything; I went over to her chair, placed opposite me at the table, and pulled it out for her. 'Good evening, little star. Won't you sit down?'

Her expression was cool and detached, yet I could see the glitter in her eyes.

She might act like one of the diamonds her company sold all she liked, but we both knew she wasn't one, not with that white fire burning away inside her.

I left her with no choice but to sit, which I knew must have annoyed her, but she only gave me a cool glance and said nothing as she came over to the chair and sat down.

I pushed her chair in, indulging myself by pausing a moment to look down at her and breathe in her sweet scent. I very much wanted to sweep aside her hair, expose the nape of her neck and bend to kiss it, but I restrained myself.

Now was not the right time.

Once she was settled, I went to the ice bucket, grabbed the champagne and popped the cork before pouring us each a glass.

Or at least, I tried to.

Olivia put her hand over the top of her glass and stared up at me, her gaze challenging. 'No wine. I want answers, Valentin. And you said you'd give them to me.'

Oh, so she was going to play it like that, was she? Interesting.

I had to admit, as much as I loved her fiery passion, a part of me was also beginning to find this new cool and imperious Olivia rather fascinating too.

In fact, both aspects of her were exciting, and I wanted to find out more.

'I said I'd give them to you over dinner,' I said mildly. 'And we haven't eaten yet.'

'I don't want dinner. I'm not hungry. Plus, I never agreed to that.'

Of course she was hungry. My staff had told me she hadn't eaten all day.

But, if she wanted a fight, I'd give her one.

I smiled, took her hand off the glass and poured champagne into it anyway—she didn't have to drink it. Then I placed the bottle back into the ice-bucket and sat down. 'You are hungry. You haven't eaten a single thing since we left Spain.'

'There is no "we", Valentin. Stop talking as if you didn't kidnap me from Domingo's wake.'

I ignored that. 'No one's forcing you to eat and no one's forcing you to drink that glass of champagne, either. If you don't want to for pettiness' sake, then I'm certainly not going to deprive you. Nothing wrong with a bit of pettiness.'

Her expression became even colder. 'I'm not being petty.'

'Are you not? Isn't that why you're refusing to eat any of the food my staff prepared for you?'

I could see the delicate line of her jaw harden in that stubborn way she had. Once, on our little beach, I'd tried to teach her the best way to start a fire. I'd just read a book on it and knew all about it. She'd refused to listen, telling me she already knew how do to it, and had insisted that her way was best even after I'd pointed out the many reasons she was wrong. She had been stubborn and wouldn't back down, and in the end we'd lit two fires at opposite ends of the beach.

She'd been right, though. Her way had been the best and the quickest.

'I'm not playing any more games with you, Valentin,' she said flatly. 'Tell me what you want and what you're going to do with me.'

'Well, I would.' I picked up my champagne and took a sip. 'But, you see, now you owe me.'

Her fair brows snapped together. 'What?'

'You slapped me, Livvy. And, granted, it didn't hurt, but still. You raised a hand to me, which means now you owe me.'

She didn't look away. 'If you're expecting an apology, you won't get it. You thoroughly deserved it. In fact, you're lucky I didn't wring your neck.'

Something intense and fierce sparked deep inside me, something that thoroughly enjoyed the uncompromising look she was giving me. Something that was finding this hard edge of hers extremely exciting and wanted to see more of it.

Had she always been like this? Certainly when we were children she'd sometimes hold a grudge for days and refuse to speak to me. Though it was true that, even when she was angry with me, she'd still come to the beach every day, even if it was only to sit on the sand and angrily throw shells into the sea. She'd known how much it meant to me to see her and she'd come anyway.

I nodded. 'I'm not apologising for bringing you here, either. So, no apologies all round.'

I knew it would infuriate her and, sure

enough, I could see her temper flicker into life, glittering behind her diamond-hard veneer.

Except…she didn't look much like a diamond now.

She looked soft and pink in that pretty silk dress, with the breeze toying gently with the ends of her hair. It was only her expression that was hard.

Perhaps tonight I'd try and shatter that veneer of hers. Perhaps tonight I'd let that fire out.

'Wonderful,' she said coldly. 'Now we've cleared that up, you can tell me what on earth you think I owe you.'

There were many things I could have said, because there were many things I wanted, and mostly from her. But all I said was, 'A sip of that champagne. Just one. It's delicious, I promise you.'

She eyed me. 'Oh, for God's sake. You never give up, do you?'

I shrugged. 'No.'

She snorted, but picked up the glass and took a sip.

I watched her. It was a very good bottle—vintage. Her favourite. She kept her expression detached as she took a sip, but then she took another, which pleased me.

I let her see that too. 'I'm glad you like it.'

I sat back in my chair. 'And now for some of those answers you wanted.'

She narrowed her gaze, but didn't put her glass back down.

'It wasn't a kidnapping,' I went on. 'It was a rescue. I had to get you away from Constantine as quickly as I could.'

'Why? What makes you think that—?'

'Because Domingo Silvera was a psychopath and, while Constantine didn't start out as one, I'm pretty sure he's one now.'

She blinked, a ripple of emotion crossing her face, though what it was I couldn't tell, since it vanished the next second. 'A psychopath? What are you talking about?'

Perhaps it was surprise. If so, I didn't blame her. Domingo preferred to keep his…tendencies veiled. People were afraid of him, and there had been certain rumours about him, but no one knew the truth.

When I was a boy, I'd used to dream that someone would realise what a monster he was and have the police come to take him away. But that had never happened. Domingo had known how to be normal, how to charm. He'd had the looks and forceful personality that could combine into a relentless charisma that blinded everyone he met. He could appear on the surface a handsome, successful, charming man, while underneath he was the devil himself.

'Constantine's father—' I could never admit to him having been mine too, because 'father' assumed a certain relationship that we'd definitely never had '—was an abusive monster and Constantine models himself on him.'

Olivia's delicate features betrayed nothing, but she'd gone a tad pale. 'That's not true. I mean, Domingo wasn't an easy man, but—'

'I won't go into the details,' I interrupted, because she didn't need to hear them. 'Suffice to say that, when I heard of your engagement, I had to take action.'

'But—'

'Domingo forbade me to see you, did you know that? But I did anyway. And eventually he found out.'

No need to tell her about Constantine's betrayal, either. That was between him and me. 'He was very angry.' I ignored the ice that coiled in my stomach at the memory. 'I decided I'd had enough by that stage, so I managed to escape. I was given a ride in a car from a stranger, but it was a wet night and he was driving too fast, and we crashed. I managed to get out, but he didn't. He was killed. Some of my DNA was found at the scene and it was assumed his body was mine. And I decided to stay dead, because if Domingo had ever discovered I was still alive he'd have followed me to the ends of the earth.'

This time, Olivia said nothing.

I still remembered that night: the skid of tyres and the smell of petrol; the sound of breaking glass and tearing metal. I'd managed to drag myself out of the car just before it had exploded and realised, in a sudden burst of relief, that if I played it right I could finally be free...

'That's why I died,' I said. 'I had to get away from Domingo. But I was afraid of what he might do to you, since he told me he'd hurt you if I disobeyed him. That's why I've been watching you all these years. I needed to protect you from him.' I took a sip of wine, my mouth oddly dry. 'And now I have to protect you from Constantine too.'

Olivia continued to stare at me, emotions flickering over her face so fast, I couldn't read them. Then abruptly she looked down at the table top and took a sip of her wine.

'I don't know anything about Domingo,' she said after a moment. 'Though, I've never felt... easy around him. And what you had to do... I'm sorry about that.' She looked up at me, her gaze again very direct. 'But you're wrong about Constantine. He's not like that.'

I just looked back at her. 'That's what everyone said about Domingo.'

'You've been gone for fifteen years, Valentin. But I've known Constantine very well for six months. I'm his fiancée. He's *not* what you think he is.'

'You're assuming,' I pointed out, 'That I haven't been watching him the same way I've been watching you. There's a reason I'm going to have him removed as CEO of Silver Inc. I'm sure he'll think it's because I want the company, but I don't. I have my own money, as you can see. No, I have to protect his employees from him somehow.'

But she didn't back down. 'That's ridiculous. Have you any evidence that he's…what? A psychopath? A cruel monster? He's cold, yes, and driven. And he's a ruthless businessman. But he's never hurt me. He's never even been rude.'

It was true that I didn't have hard evidence that Constantine was exactly like Domingo. I'd never found any rumours that he'd been physically violent or manipulative the way Domingo had been.

But he was cruel and callous and ruthless. Detached and cold and utterly without empathy. His staff were afraid of him, or so my mole had told me, and that was likely due to him holding something over their heads. It had been Domingo's favourite method of maintaining obedience, even though it had never worked on me, and I was sure Constantine employed it too.

'Yes,' I said. 'That's what he wants you to think. He's exactly like Domingo, though. And, while I haven't spent the past fifteen years with him, I grew up with him and I know exactly what goes on in his head.' *You did. Once.* I ignored the thought and smiled. 'I'm his twin, after all.'

But Olivia was shaking her head. 'You're wrong. And, apart from anything else, this is ridiculous. Keeping me here is ridiculous. What are you going to do with me? You can't keep me here for ever.'

'I don't need to keep you here for ever.' I held her gaze and let her see the force of my will. 'All I need to do is keep you here long enough for you to fall in love with me. And then you'll marry me instead. Like you always wanted to.'

CHAPTER SEVEN

Olivia

VALENTIN'S BLACK EYES glittered in the light from the candles in the hurricane lamps. There was nothing but fierce certainty in his hard, carved features.

Maybe it's not Constantine you should be afraid of. Maybe it's him.

But I wasn't afraid of Constantine, and I certainly wasn't afraid of Valentin. I was angry, yes, but not afraid.

The air was warm and soft and smelled of flowers, the light from all those pretty candles dancing over the wood of the jetty and casting a lovely glow. The only sound was of the waves lapping against the jetty supports.

The table and the silver service, the crystal glass full of champagne, the tropical setting… it was all so beautiful.

And so was the man sitting across from me

in jeans and bare feet, lounging at his ease, his champagne glass held loosely in his long fingers. His black hair was tousled and the white of his T-shirt made his olive skin look darker, all smooth and velvety. It highlighted the darkness of his eyes and, even though they were so black they were like space, I could see the lights in them, flames burning.

Domingo was a monster and Valentin had been forbidden to see me. Domingo had threatened to hurt me. Valentin had faked his own death to escape him. I could hardly believe it. Or, no; maybe I could believe it.

I'd never liked Domingo. He had been charming but there'd been something about him, a kind of clinical detachment that had always made me uneasy.

But Valentin was wrong about Constantine. Yes, Constantine was cold, but he'd never made me uneasy in the way Domingo had. And he'd never been cruel, never hurt me in any way. And then there was Jenny, his stepsister, who worshipped the ground he walked on. Jenny, who was always so smiley and happy and cheerful. She'd never be that loyal to a monster.

But as for what Valentin had said, about keeping me here and me falling in love with him and him marrying me instead…

Something tugged deep inside me. A longing I thought I'd got rid of years ago.

But no. Marrying Valentin? What a preposterous thought. The passionate boy he'd once been had grown up, though he was obviously still passionate. But he was also arrogant, egotistical to a fault and it was clear that he'd never even heard of the word 'no'.

He was a difficult man, just like my father had been, and if there was one thing I didn't want in my life it was another difficult man.

And Constantine is easy...?

Well, no, he wasn't. But I didn't feel anything for him, I didn't have a history with him, and that made all the difference.

'You can't be serious,' I said coolly. 'Are you actually insane? What a preposterous suggestion.'

His teeth were white in the flickering light. 'Perhaps. You don't grow up in the house of a psychopath without some scars, I suppose. But does it matter that it's preposterous? For the first time in fifteen years, we're alone, Livvy. And there's no one to stop us from being together if we want to be, not this time.'

From out of nowhere, an electric thrill shot straight down my spine, going all the way to the heart of the girl I'd once been. That ferocious girl, who'd argued and fought and played and laughed with him on that secret beach. That passionate girl who'd loved him with all of her soul.

And I'd loved being that girl. Because being with him had made me feel more like myself than anyone else ever had. I hadn't been silly or dramatic or overly emotional when I'd been with him. I'd been able to be angry without having someone tell me that I was turning everything into a big drama. I'd been able to laugh myself hoarse without being told to calm down. He accepted me and my emotions without question, and I'd loved that.

But there had been a weakness in that girl, in the end. A flaw in her supposedly strong façade. And it was the same flaw my mother had: our heart.

I'd loved a man who'd hurt me and so, no matter how much I'd loved being that girl, I'd never be her again. She'd been a child and I'd buried her when Valentin had supposedly died. I was in no hurry to resurrect her.

My instinct was to tell him he was mistaken, get to my feet and leave, but he wasn't wrong about the fact that I hadn't eaten all day. And, yes, maybe refusing to eat had been petty of me. It had certainly been a mistake. Because it was coming back to haunt me now, my stomach rumbling at the sight and smell of the delicious food that had been laid on the table.

An array of salads, fish and shellfish that had no doubt been caught in the lagoon. Newly baked bread with a thick pat of butter. It all looked so fresh and tasty, and it was everything I particularly liked to eat.

Had he known? Had he done that on purpose? Oh, but of course he'd known, and of course he'd done it on purpose. He'd just said he wanted me to fall in love with him, and I suppose this was the start of his seduction.

Which meant that, naturally, I couldn't eat any of it.

Valentin put his wine down and leaned forward, his elbows on the table. 'There's dessert too.' His eyes danced, full of the wickedness and delight I'd always found so irresistible. 'I have marshmallows. We can build a fire on the beach and toast them.'

Instantly I was back on that beach again, arguing with him about the best way to build a driftwood fire. He'd been as stubborn as me and insistent that his way was the right way. We'd been twelve. I'd told him he was a dumb boy who knew nothing. He'd told me I was a stupid girl who knew even less. Then he'd kicked sand in my direction while I'd thrown a stick at him. Then we'd gone off to opposite ends of the beach and lit fires to prove each other wrong.

Valentin's rages had never lasted long. They'd

been intense while they lasted but, like a hurricane, they'd blown themselves out quickly. I'd held on to mine much longer, unwilling to let them go.

But that day on the beach Val had eventually come across to look at my fire and he'd smiled suddenly; it had been like the dawn breaking. 'That's amazing, Livvy,' he'd said, as if he hadn't called me a stupid girl and kicked sand at me not minutes before. 'I couldn't even get a flame.'

Once his anger had gone, he hadn't cared about being right. And that day we'd sat beside the fire I'd successfully lit and toasted marshmallows together.

'You can build the fire,' Valentin murmured. 'You're good at building fires, as I recall.'

The thing that had tugged in my chest tugged again. Painfully. Something that felt like yearning.

But I shoved it away. Hard.

I wasn't going there. I wasn't. I couldn't. Not again.

I took a breath and met his gaze, feeling myself as consumed by it as I always had been. 'I'm not lighting fires with you, Valentin. And thank you for the meal. I'm sure it's lovely, and I appreciate the effort, but I'm not sitting out here and reminiscing with you about old times.'

I gripped the glass of champagne and raised it, swallowing the whole of it down, because it was delicious and I needed it; and because, even after all this time, I still found it difficult to walk away from him. 'But I'm not the same person I was back then. That girl you knew... She's gone. I'm not falling in love with you, and I'm certainly not marrying you, understand?'

I got to my feet, the champagne glittering in my bloodstream, and reached for a roll. 'I'll take this for my dinner. But that's all. Thank you for the wine.'

Valentin didn't move. 'So you're running away now?'

'Hardly.' I turned and stepped away from the table.

'You ran from everyone else, but you never ran from me. Don't you remember?' His voice was quiet, yet I heard.

I stopped a few steps away from the table and, even though I hated myself for stopping, something inside wouldn't let me take another step.

'You didn't want me at your beach, remember?' he went on in the same quiet voice. 'I could tell. You were sitting there, enjoying the silence, and then suddenly this rowdy boy appeared. You wanted to leave, and you hated me for disturbing your special place, but for some reason you stayed.'

I remembered. I had been ten and my parents had had a fight, filling the house with my father's cold fury and my mother's weepy apologies.

I'd hated it when they fought, when my father was so cruel and my mother just took it. It had made me angry with her, made me want to yell at her to fight back. But I knew that would only make it worse, so I'd run away to the beach I'd discovered a couple of days earlier. It had been next to our villa, small, quiet and hidden by trees and cliffs, and no one had known about it. No one but me.

Valentin was right, though. I'd been enjoying the silence until this black-eyed, older boy had appeared. I'd hated him instantly for disturbing me, for finding my special beach and ruining it with his presence. And I'd been on the point of getting up and leaving when something magical had happened.

Unlike me, the boy hadn't been annoyed to find someone else there. No, his face had lit up, as if my being there had been the best thing that had ever happened to him. And his smile had been incandescent. He'd looked at me as if I were magic. As if I were incredible. As if I wasn't the constant reminder of my mother's failure to give her husband a son and treated accordingly by both my parents. My father had always been coldly impatient with me, my mother constantly anxious that I would do something to offend him.

'Don't go,' he'd said, as if sensing I was about to leave. 'Please stay.'

Even then I'd been able to see he was like a bonfire, intense and burning, holding me mesmerised. My father had been cold, my mother soft and floaty and ineffectual, but this boy had been…intense. And I had been drawn to his intensity like a moth to a flame.

No. I'd never run from him.

So why are you walking away now?

'Are you afraid of me?' Valentin's voice was low and deep, winding around me like a velvet rope. 'Did I scare you with all that talk of monsters and psychopaths?'

My heart was beating far too fast, and I didn't want him to come near me. Something might happen if he did. Something I wasn't sure I'd to be able to come back from.

So? Keep walking.

But I didn't.

Instead, I gave him a mocking look. 'Afraid? Of you? Seriously?'

He ignored my tone. 'Well, you have no guarantee I'm not as mad as Domingo. And I can't say for certain I'm not. But, no, perhaps it's not me you're afraid of. Perhaps it's yourself.'

I shouldn't have turned round then. I should have kept right on walking. Yet once again I stayed where I was.

The breeze lifted the silken skirts of my dress, the silk brushing against my skin making me very aware that all I wore beneath it was that tiny bikini.

'I think not,' I said icily, desperately trying to keep my cool.

Valentin didn't move, still lounging in his chair, yet the flames in his eyes leapt high. He was so fierce, so intense. So bright. He was the brightest thing I'd ever seen, and he still was.

'Aren't you, though? Isn't that why you're walking away?' He put down his wine and shoved his chair back, getting to his feet in one smooth, powerful movement. 'If I got close to you now, what would you do? Run away?' He came towards me unhurriedly, as if he had all the time in the world. 'Or stand your ground the way you used to?'

Something was bubbling up inside me, the fury I thought I'd put on a leash earlier that day. Fury at the impossible choice he'd given me, because walking away now would reveal far too much. Yet standing my ground was exactly what he wanted me to do.

It was all his talk of the past, of course. Somehow, he'd used that to reach inside me, bypassing my diamond armour and touching the soul of the girl I'd once been.

He'd manipulated me and I'd let him.

My father had always hated open, uncontrolled anger. It was a sign of weak character, he'd said. And, because I wasn't weak I'd never got angry. I'd only gone cold.

But I wasn't cold now. That fury was welling up inside me and I couldn't control it. Fury at him for reminding me of who I'd once been, for taking those old yearnings and desires and making me want them again. For putting me in this impossible position, where I could be a coward, like my mother doing whatever my father told her.

And, most of all, fury at myself for allowing myself to let him do this to me.

He was still coming towards me and the edge of the jetty was near.

So I didn't wait. I had to do something.

I took two steps, gave him a hard shove and pushed him off the edge into the sea.

CHAPTER EIGHT

Valentin

I KNEW WHAT she was going to do. If nothing else, those long summers on our beach had taught me that when Olivia was going to push me, shove me or throw something at me, she'd dart a glance round at her surroundings, as if to check no one was watching.

To be fair, I had been expecting another slap in the face, not a hard shove into the ocean—though, given how close the edge of the jetty was, I certainly should have predicted it. Especially when this wasn't the first time she'd pushed me into the sea.

She used to do it quite regularly, as if she couldn't help herself. I'd be innocently exploring some rock pools on our beach and out would come her arm, giving me a push. It was a game we'd played and, since it had made her laugh, and I'd loved making her laugh, I'd let her push me far more than was necessary.

She hadn't even minded when I'd pulled her in too. In fact, she'd laughed the last time I'd done it.

She wasn't laughing now, though, as I grabbed her just before I went over, a reflex I couldn't stop. But then, perhaps I wouldn't have stopped even if I could have. I wanted her to remember what we'd had together, all those bright days on the beach, playing and laughing together.

Domingo had policed the contact Constantine and I had had with other people. We hadn't been allowed friends or acquaintances. But he'd relaxed his guard on our Caribbean holidays and so I'd been able to slip away to the beach.

Olivia had been my first and only friend and, despite all the years that had passed and all the things I'd done to get where I was now, she was still the only one.

She'd always be the only one.

The only one for me.

So I pulled her in with me and she shrieked in outrage as we fell into the sea, the water as warm as a bath. Her skirts wrapped around my legs and her hair was everywhere, and there was a moment where she was obviously struggling to orient herself.

I was an excellent swimmer, so I held her in my arms as I found my feet on the sandy ocean floor, taking care to make sure she didn't swallow any water as we surfaced.

She was furious, yet her hands clutched onto my shoulders, as if holding on for dear life. Her eyes were brilliant in the flickering light from the candles in the hurricane lamps, sea water like jewels on her skin. Her hair streamed over her shoulders, the ends floating in long, silky skeins on the surface.

She was so beautiful, she stopped my heart.

Then she hit me hard on the shoulder. 'You pulled me in. That was so unfair!'

She sounded just like she had all those years ago, when I'd won whatever game we'd been playing, often accusing me of being unfair or cheating. And sometimes I had been.

But her fury had been just as mesmerising to me as her laughter, so I did what I'd wanted to do so many times on that beach long ago.

I bent and covered her mouth with mine.

I remembered our first kiss. It had been mine too, since naturally enough, if Domingo had forbidden Constantine and me friends, he'd always forbidden us girlfriends. I'd never held a girl before, never kissed one either, and it had been so very, very sweet.

I could still taste that sweetness. It was still

there. But we weren't fifteen and seventeen any longer, and a very real, very adult heat leapt between us now.

It was electric.

Women had long since beaten a path to my bed and I'd lost count of those I'd taken. After all, sex was one of life's pleasures and I'd never denied myself.

But Olivia had always been different, and kissing her was as different from kissing all those other women as night was from day.

She tasted of champagne and sea salt, of sex and desire, and I wanted her now, right now. I was tired of waiting and I wanted it all.

She went rigid in my arms, her whole body taut and, even though it was the last thing on earth I wanted, I forced myself to let her go.

I'd given her a taste. If she wanted more, she knew where to get it.

Olivia stared at me, her brilliant grey eyes full of fury. But I could see the desire there too, burning hot. She looked as though she wasn't sure whether to kiss me or strangle me.

I didn't look away and I said nothing. I let her make the choice.

Then suddenly she lunged forward, her arms winding around my neck, her hot, slender body arching against me as her mouth found mine.

Triumph filled me just before all thought

shattered. Triumph that she'd made her choice and her choice was me. And then there was only her in my arms. Her, after so many years of watching her from the shadows, wanting her but trying not to. Dreaming of her and losing her every morning when I woke up.

But not now. Now she was here and she wasn't a dream. She was reality and she was finally where she'd always belonged: in my arms.

I could taste the fire inside her now, and I dug my fingers into the wet silk of her hair, pulling her head back so I could kiss her deeper, harder, chase that taste. Her mouth was so hot and she was trying to kiss me back, her tongue touching mine, at first tentatively, and then with more confidence, more passion.

She kissed like a virgin, which only sharpened the edge of my hunger. I'd suspected Constantine hadn't taken her to bed and this confirmed it.

She was mine. Every part of her was mine. And something inside me regretted all the women I'd taken to my bed over the years…regretted that she was not my first, my only. That I wasn't all hers the way she would be mine.

But there was nothing I could do about that now.

I might have had many other women physically, but my heart was pure. My heart had always been hers.

I kissed her with savagery, with demand and, because she was Olivia, she kissed me back the same way, her arms tight around my neck, her slender curves pressed hard to the entire length of my body.

The sea washed around us, swirling the silk of her dress around my legs, making me aware of all the clothes between us and how I didn't want them to be there. I wanted nothing between us, just her bare skin and the heat of her mouth. The tight clasp of her sex around me as I pushed inside her and made her mine.

I tore my mouth from hers and began to kiss my way down the slender column of her throat, tasting the salt water and sweetness of her skin.

Her head dropped back, the sound of her breathing ragged in the night air.

I fastened my mouth over her pulse, tasting the frantic beat of it with my tongue, and she shuddered, a soft moan escaping her.

Yes, I wanted more of that sound. More of her, a slave to this heat between us. I wanted to make her cry for me, beg for me; I wanted her as desperate as she'd made me.

I pulled hard at the neckline of her dress, silk tearing to reveal the lavender bikini top she wore beneath it. The last of the summer sunset had disappeared, her skin now glowing like mother-of-pearl in the starlight, and I wanted to see it. I wanted to see all of it.

I jerked the strap of her bikini top down, un-covering one round breast, and she gasped as I slid my palm around it, cupping her.

Dios, she was perfect. As perfect as I'd imag-ined. Her skin was silky-smooth and hot, her rosy-pink nipple hard and ready for my mouth.

I dipped my head, hungry for more of a taste, tracing the curve of her breast with my tongue and then circling that hard little peak.

'Val…' Her voice was husky and thick in the night, her fingers digging into my shoulders. 'Oh… Val…'

I teased her, then drew her nipple into my mouth, sucking hard, and she cried out.

It was the sweetest sound I'd ever heard. Just as she was the sweetest thing I'd ever tasted.

I gripped her hips, fitting her more closely against me. My heart was racing and the ache in my groin was insistent. I was harder than I'd ever been in my entire life.

But I didn't want her here in the water. I wanted her somewhere I could lay her out and tear those clothes away completely, have her naked under the stars. Somewhere more comfortable, where I could feast on her at my leisure.

Of course, the perfect place wasn't that far away.

I tore my mouth from her breast and lifted her, urging her to wrap her legs around my waist, because I didn't want to lose contact with her. She didn't hesitate, her arms looping around my neck, those delectable breasts soft and hot pressed to my chest.

She found my mouth, kissing me desperately as I turned towards the beach and began wading through the water. I let her explore, since I knew what she was doing.

She didn't want me to stop, because if I stopped this now she'd start to think. It would come back to her where she was and who I was and what we were doing. And that diamond-hard veneer of hers would come back down. The white-star heat of her would get locked away.

Well. Luckily for us both, I wasn't going to let that happen.

I waded out of the water and onto the little beach, the jetty stretching out beside us. The sand was still warm from the day, glowing white under the stars.

I let Olivia go and then I pushed her down onto the sand on her back, spreading her thighs with my hands so I could kneel between them.

Then I ripped the silk dress from her body.

She trembled but didn't stop me, her eyes wide as they stared up into mine. I could see starlight reflected in them and the white heat blazing at the heart of her.

I leaned down, kissing her hard and deep, because I didn't want that sharp brain of hers thinking; I didn't want her having second thoughts.

This was where we needed to be for our first time together—on a beach, on the sand, at night.

So I kept on kissing her as I pulled away her bikini and she was finally where she always should have been.

Naked, beneath me.

CHAPTER NINE

Olivia

I COULDN'T BREATHE. I couldn't think. My heart felt as if it was going to beat its way out of my chest.

My skin was hot and far too tight, and I wanted to cast it off and crawl out of it like a butterfly from a cocoon. So I felt nothing but relief when Valentin tore off my dress and then the bikini beneath it.

The sand beneath me was soft and warm, but that was nothing compared to the heat of the man who knelt between my thighs. He gripped his soaking-wet T-shirt and tore it up and over his head in one smooth, powerful movement. And all I could do was stare at him as he flung it away.

From his wide shoulders, the water glistened along every hard, carved muscle of his torso. I'd seen it already, of course, but this was different. Now I could touch him, now I could run my hands over all the expanse of tanned skin and see if it felt as velvety and as smooth as it looked.

Dimly, something in the back of my head shouted a warning—that I was forgetting myself. That I shouldn't let this happen. That this was a step I couldn't come back from—but I ignored it.

As soon as he'd pulled me after him into the sea, I knew my fate had been sealed. Because his strong hands gripped me, and the warm water of the ocean closed around me, and I was back on that hidden beach again. Laughing at him as I pushed him into the water. Squealing as he splashed me, then shrieking as he pulled me in too.

My heart would burst as I surfaced to find him bobbing in the water next to me, his black hair hanging over his forehead, his dark eyes full of wickedness and the sheer joy of being alive.

'Stand on my shoulders,' he'd say, holding out his arms. 'I'll throw you.'

So I had, feeling the power in those strong shoulders even then, even back when he was seventeen. Then he'd gripped my ankles and crouched down in the water before surging back up, releasing me to leap high into the sky, as high as I could get before splashing back down.

I'd felt as if I were flying.

I felt as if I were flying now.

There was no need for armour, no need for the icy control I cultivated. There was only him and the desire I could no longer fight.

I sat up, desperate to touch him, reaching out for his wet skin, feeling heat and hard muscle. I shook with desire, with desperation, because I'd never touched a man's bare torso like this, and I couldn't believe how hungry it made me.

I'd never felt such desire for a man. I'd never felt desire at all for anyone, not even Constantine.

He looked like Valentin, but people had always been wrong in thinking that they were identical. They weren't. Constantine hadn't thrown me into the sky. Constantine hadn't argued with me about the best way to build a fire. Constantine hadn't held me in the darkness and kissed me and told me he loved me.

'Ah, little star,' Valentin whispered, taking my hands away from his body and kissing my fingertips the way he'd used to do. 'No touching. Not yet.'

'I don't care,' I whispered back. 'Let me.'

'No.' And, before I could protest further, he pressed me back down, taking my wrists in one

strong hand and pinning them to the sand above
my head. He stared down at me, his expression fierce, blazing with intensity as he reached
down with his free hand to undo his jeans.

The warning in my head sounded again, but
I didn't listen.

I didn't want to.

I knew what he was going to do and I couldn't
think of anything I wanted more, because it was
perfect like this. On the beach, in the dark,
under the stars.

'Estrella,' he murmured, the Spanish lilting
and musical, and then something else, something I didn't understand.

I began to tremble as his hand settled on my
bare stomach, his gaze on mine, and then he
stroked me and every one of my senses came
alive. His fingers were hot, a brand on my damp
skin, and the ache between my legs suddenly
felt like more than I could bear.

Every inch of my body wanted his touch, his
hands, his mouth, his tongue. And I couldn't
stop myself from arching up, from offering myself to him.

'Please,' I moaned.

'You want me, Livvy?' His hand slid down,
his fingers grazing the curls between my thighs
and making me shiver all over. 'Tell me. Say it.'

I shouldn't do what he said, yet I didn't even

think of disobeying him. 'Yes, I want you. I want you now, please.'

'My name, little star.' His voice deepened, became a growl. 'Say my name.'

'Valentin…' I sighed, his name escaping like a prayer. 'I want you, Val.'

His hand moved, sliding down further, touching me where I was most sensitive, where I ached and ached and ached.

I shuddered as his fingertips struck sparks of pleasure along every nerve-ending I had, stroking through the folds of my sex, gently exploring me. A gasp escaped me and I shut my eyes as pleasure bloomed.

But then he said, 'No, don't close your eyes. Look at me, Livvy. Look only at me.'

So I did, staring upwards into his beautiful face. Because he was beautiful; he always had been. And, despite what I'd told myself all these years, I'd missed him so much. When I'd heard he'd died, a part of me had been ripped away.

He wasn't gone any more, though. He was here. He was right here with me, his gaze on mine, all velvet darkness, but not wholly black. Not completely. I'd never realised till now, but there were stars in his eyes, light glittering deep in all that shadow. I couldn't look away.

His fingers shifted, sliding inside me, and I groaned as the pleasure spread out, engulfing me like the sea. Then he took his hand away and put his mouth there instead and I burst into flames like a bonfire.

He explored me with his tongue, licking insistently, his hands holding my hips to the sand as I writhed in an agony of pleasure. I reached down and buried my fingers in his damp black hair, crying out his name as he continued to taste me with a single-minded relentlessness that had me losing my grip on reality.

There was nothing but the fire of his touch and the black sky above me; the heat of his mouth and the pleasure that threatened to consume me. He pushed me to the brink with that magic tongue of his and then, when he pushed it inside me, he sent me over the edge and I cried out as the orgasm crashed over me, ecstasy glittering in my bloodstream like the stars above, making me shake, gasp and tremble.

Then he rose above me as I lay there panting in the sand and got rid of his sodden jeans and underwear. Naked, he looked like a god…a sea god…all wet skin, sleek seal-dark hair and glittering black eyes. His body looked as if it was carved from rock, taut and hard, and so hot that when he covered me I felt as if I'd been burned.

I reached to touch him, still trembling from that orgasm, but he shook his head, pinning my wrists again, holding me down. The expression on his face was so intense it took my breath away…so fierce. As if I were a prize he'd fought long and hard for which now he could finally claim. Finally, I was his.

It was thrilling to be looked at like that, because I'd been the irritating girl-child with all her various flaws. Reluctantly given a company I didn't deserve when, really, both my parents would much rather have had a boy.

But I'd never been a disappointment to Val. Not even that first day we met, when he'd appeared on the beach and his eyes had lit up.

'Don't go. Please stay.'

My heart throbbed, a raw, heavy emotion gathering in my chest.

'Val,' I whispered, not even sure what I wanted to say to him, only that I felt something huge, something without a name, and it scared me. And it was because of him.

He said nothing, just watched me as I felt the heat of his bare skin shifting against me as he nudged between my thighs. His gaze burned, full of a raw heat that made my mouth go dry, and then I felt the head of his sex push against me, then into me.

I was so wet, there was no resistance and no pain. Only the intense sensation of my body stretching to accommodate his, clasping him tightly as if he was something I couldn't bear to let go.

I gasped aloud because, even though it didn't hurt, it was still a shock…and he was big. Were all men this big? I could hardly breathe for the pressure.

My fingertips dug into his powerful shoulders and I gasped again as he sank deeper, his free hand sliding under me, lifting me, tilting me so he could go even deeper.

'Yes, Olivia…' he growled, his voice rough and guttural, black eyes blazing down at me in triumph. 'You're mine now. You're *all* mine.'

Then he bent and kissed me hard and deep, conquering me, mastering me so completely that all I could do was surrender.

But maybe that was always what I'd meant to do with Val. I'd always meant to surrender to him.

Then every thought in my head fractured and broke apart as he began to move, at first slow and easy, and then faster, harder. He was relentless and powerful and I tried to move with him, arching and straining against the hold he had on my wrists.

But he didn't let me go, making me take whatever he gave until the sheer ecstasy of it consumed me whole.

I lost myself in the ferocity of his kiss. In the

slide of him inside me, the exquisite friction of it driving me on past pleasure and into something deeper and more intense. Something that was made up of his kiss, his touch and the scent of salt and cinnamon. The heat of his body and the rough sound of his voice.

The beat of his heart and the way he said my name.

And then, at the end the sheer rush of pleasure that exploded inside me, he launched me off his shoulders and into the sky. Making me fly, the way he always had.

CHAPTER TEN

Valentin

I HEARD OLIVIA scream my name and felt her body convulse, her sex tightening around mine as the orgasm took her. And I let go of the leash I had on myself, moving inside her hard and deep, tasting her sweet mouth, covering myself in her passion, letting myself burn.

I couldn't make it last, though. I'd wanted her too much and for too long, and the scent and feel of her, the sound of her husky voice pleading for me, just about made me lose my mind.

The orgasm came for me far too quickly, an intense rush of pleasure that shot up my spine and exploded in my brain like a firework. Then my head was full of stars and, looking down into her eyes, they were all I could see...all those stars glittering in her eyes.

For long moments we stared at each other and I was conscious of every little thing about her: the glow of perspiration on her forehead; the pout of her kiss-swollen lips; the damp strands of hair stuck to her forehead; the deep flush in her cheeks; the frantic beat of her pulse at her throat.

Finally, she was mine.

And I wasn't letting her go.

A deep, intense satisfaction filled me, and I shifted, deciding that it was time we swapped the beach for somewhere more comfortable. She made a soft sound as I withdrew from her that sent a rush of yet more heat through me, but I restrained myself, settling for picking her up in my arms and carrying her down into the sea to wash the sand from us both.

She lay quietly against my chest, the warmth of her naked body making me hard again, staring up at me as if she'd never seen me before in her life.

I didn't say anything and neither did she, the silence settling around us as the warm seawater got rid of the sand.

'We shouldn't have done that,' she said at last, her voice slightly hoarse.

It might have annoyed me if I'd thought she meant it, but I knew she didn't. Because of course we should have done that. It was *exactly* what we should have done. It had been perfect—everything I'd dreamed about and more.

I glanced down at her. Her eyes had darkened and I could see that she wanted some confirmation from me, though why I wasn't sure. No; perhaps I did know why.

She was afraid. Afraid of the intensity between us. It made me aware yet again of how she'd changed, of how cool and hard she'd become. She'd always embraced her passions as a girl, yet from my observations of her now, and over the past few years as I'd watched her, it was clear that she didn't embrace them now.

Why? What had happened to make her so afraid? Was it her father? Managing that company she helmed?

Oliver Wintergreen had never wanted a girl, or so she'd told me once. He'd only wanted a boy, and so her mother had always tried to make her more acceptable to him, while her father had got impatient with what he saw as her 'girlish tantrums and drama'.

I'd never understood how they couldn't see what they had in her. She felt things very deeply and had a strong sense of justice and fairness. She also had a ridiculous sense of humour, and was fearless, yet had the most compassionate heart. She was perfect in every way, and I'd thought them as mad as Domingo in their own way, and just as blind.

'Why not?' I let the water lap up around her,

my gaze dropping to her breasts, fascinated by how the cool touch of the sea made her nipples go hard.

'So many reasons.' She made no move to cover herself, her body relaxed and warm against mine. 'We didn't use a condom, either.'

A chill stole through me. I'd never forgotten protection, not once, since the thought of children was appalling to me. After all, who wanted to pass down the defective Silvera genes? Certainly I didn't.

'I'll call the doctor.' I kept my tone very casual. 'We'll handle it.'

The dazed look on her face began to dissipate and I could feel her body start to stiffen in my arms. 'What do you mean, "we'll handle it"?'

'I mean the morning-after pill. Children can't be part of this, Olivia.'

She stared up at me a moment and I could see it happen. I could see the softness leaching out of her, the hard veneer coming back down like a security screen in a bank. 'And what if…?'

But I didn't want to continue with this particular subject, so I made her break off in a gasp, sliding my hand up to cup one round breast, her skin slippery from the water. I teased her nipple gently with my thumb, feeling it get even harder beneath my touch.

'And what if…what?' I asked lazily, circling her nipple and squeezing her lightly.

She trembled in my arms. 'Don't…do that.'

'Why not? You like it.'

And I could see that she did, her head falling back against my shoulder, hunger darkening in her eyes. 'We need to…talk.'

'You don't want to talk, little star.' I pinched her nipple and she jerked, a groan escaping her. 'You want me to keep doing this.'

'I…don't…' Yet even as she said it her back arched and she pressed herself into my hand.

'We'll have time to talk later.' I dropped my head, brushing my mouth over hers, feeling her lips open beneath mine. 'Plenty of time…'

She had no response to that other than to kiss me harder, which soon brought our little chat to a close.

I carried her out of the water and took her back into the villa. Then I ran some warm water into the big white bath in the bathroom and washed us both clean. I teased her in the bath, tantalised her, stroked every inch of her body; and only when she was gasping, trembling and begging did I lift her out, dry her off and take her back to my bed.

I made love to her again, this time taking things slowly, exploring every inch of her so that all she was thinking of when I finally pushed inside her was me and the pleasure I was giving her.

After we'd both recovered she was ravenous, because of course she'd had nothing to eat all day, so we wandered back down the jetty to the table. The food wasn't any the worse for wear, and I insisted she sit in my lap so I could feed her little morsels of whatever she fancied.

Or at least, I tried to insist. She was adamant that wasn't happening, so I'd decided not to force the issue, as the last couple of times I'd forced it, it hadn't ended well for me.

A good choice, as it turned out, when five minutes later she changed her mind and sat regally in my lap as if I were her favourite chair.

It satisfied something deep in me to take care of her like this, as it had all those years ago when I'd managed to toast the perfect marshmallow for her, handing it to her with ceremony. The pleasure of watching her eat it had been... indescribable.

I'd never had anything of my own to take care of before. Constantine and I hadn't been allowed pets. Nothing we might form emotional attachments to. We'd only had each other, and even then Domingo hadn't liked it.

He had driven a wedge between us, and I had let it happen, because I hadn't wanted Constantine to follow my lead. I was his older brother, if only by a few minutes, and I was supposed to protect him, so protect him I had. His safety had depended on him being Domingo's favourite and that was what I'd made sure he was. By making myself Domingo's target.

Except you failed, didn't you?

But I didn't want to think about that right now, what with Olivia in my arms, so I pushed the thought away.

'Have you really been watching me all this time?' Olivia asked, lying back against my shoulder, her hair, dry now, spilling over my arm in a long, straight fall. I was only wearing a pair of jeans, so it felt like silk against my bare skin.

She was in one of those floaty dresses I'd bought especially for her, though it was more a long, filmy tunic in blue and lavender silk than a dress. It was just as transparent as all the others, which meant I could see her beautiful body through the fabric.

She didn't seem to mind this time. In fact, lying like this in my arms, well pleasured and now fed, she was nothing but passion and sensuality, her hard veneer gone.

She was magical like this.

'Not initially, no.' I wound a lock of her hair around my finger, watching the candlelight gloss it gold. 'After the car accident, it took me some time to get my resources together.'

She glanced up at me. 'What happened, Val?'

What to tell her?

Perhaps the truth?

Yes, but what truth?

I'd never cared what other people thought of me. Why would a lion concern himself with the opinions of sheep? Especially back then, in those early days after the accident, when I'd had to do what I could to survive.

But isn't that what you've always done? Whatever you have to?

There had been no other choice. My childhood had been a battleground that had left few survivors and I'd always made sure that my brother would be one of them.

'What happened?' I echoed. 'Well, like I told you, there was only one way to escape Domingo and that was to let everyone assume I was dead. So that's what I did. I managed to get into Italy and found some under-the-table work for a time. Then I...' How to put it? Would she accept that I'd fallen in with a mentor who was part of a crime network? And that I'd become one of them because I'd had nowhere else to go and no way to earn a living? Would she judge the company I'd built after taking over that crime network and turned it legitimate?

Would she judge *me*?

Dios, why did the thought of her judgement matter?

'You what?' she prompted.

I stared back at her, letting her see a bit of the truth in my eyes. 'If you're thinking mine is a plucky David Copperfield story, then you should think again.'

'I wasn't thinking that.'

Uneasiness shifted inside me. I didn't want to tell her, which was ridiculous.

She sat up in my lap all of a sudden, the silk of her tunic sliding over my skin as she faced me. Her pretty eyes were only inches away and I could see that there were still tiny grains of sand in her hairline. I liked her like this, all tumbled and ruffled, less poised and perfect.

'I think you did whatever you could to survive,' she said, lifting my own thoughts straight out of my head. 'You're a ruthless man, Val. I can see that now. And whatever you had to do, it probably wasn't easy.' She paused a moment, searching my face. 'You don't have to tell me if you don't want to.'

I didn't like that she could see so much of me, that she could read me so easily. No one else could. Then again, no one knew me the way she did.

She knew the boy. She doesn't know the man.

I stared into her grey eyes. 'I fell in with a man who ran a major crime empire in the south of Italy. Mafia connections, that kind of thing. I helped him run it and then, when he was killed in a car bomb, I took it over.'

Again, a flicker of some emotion I didn't recognise passed over her face, a shadow that made her eyes darken.

'Oh, don't worry.' I couldn't hide the edge in my voice. 'I took it all legitimate years ago. You're not soiling yourself with some evil crime lord.'

If she found the sharp note in the words an issue, she didn't show it. She only frowned. 'It doesn't matter to me what you did. I'm just sorry that you had to do it.'

I let go of her curl, lifted my hand and wound all my fingers in her hair, not liking the strange, heavy feeling of regret that sat on my chest like a stone; wanting to feel softness against my skin instead.

'I needed money and power if I wanted to protect you and that was the quickest way to get both.' I closed my hand in a fist and said both to her and to myself, 'And I don't regret it.'

CHAPTER ELEVEN

Olivia

HE DID REGRET IT. I could see it in his eyes. Whatever he'd done to get that money and that power, he hadn't wanted to do it.

My heart tightened. All the anger I'd felt towards him earlier seemed to have vanished, lost in the passion that had consumed us on the beach. Now what I felt was a hard tug of sympathy, and a growing curiosity about the life he'd led after he'd 'died'.

It hadn't been an easy one, that seemed obvious, and it had pretty much crushed the boy he'd once been. The kind, loving boy who'd once been so good to me.

Yet, had that boy been entirely stripped away? Certainly, I could see traces of him in the food he'd had made for me and the French champagne in the ice-bucket. In the way he'd gently washed me in the bath, and in the way he was holding me now.

Protectiveness had always been in his nature.

It made it difficult to tell whether all of that—the dinner, the drinks, the talk of the past—had been manipulation or whether it had been him genuinely being kind.

I didn't know. Perhaps I needed to stop thinking about that boy and start concentrating on the man.

A ruthless, charming man. Manipulative, yes, yet also driven; I could see that. However, while he seemed quite happy to talk about our past, his was a different story.

And you don't want to push him on it.

No, I didn't, not now.

We had something of a détente and, while I hadn't meant to lie here comfortably in his arms, naked but for a silky tunic, I was strangely okay with it.

I hadn't wanted to initially, finding the thought of sitting in his lap a little too much like being his plaything for comfort. But he hadn't insisted, and somehow I'd found myself changing my mind. It seemed silly not to be physically close to him after what had happened on the beach, and if I wanted it, then why not?

It was my choice and that didn't make me a doormat. Besides, as I'd told myself as he'd picked me up out of the sea and washed me carefully in the bath, what was between us was merely physical. Just pleasure, nothing more.

It didn't mean anything was going to change.

I was still engaged to Constantine, and I still fully intended to find my way back to him. Val was wrong about him, I was certain, and those debts needed paying.

I also still wanted an heir, and it was clear what Val's thoughts were on the subject. His response to the lack of a condom had been unequivocal. He did not want children.

But he'd given me the most unbelievable pleasure, and, as I knew a marriage to Constantine wouldn't give me that, why shouldn't I take this while I could?

I'd worked hard for my father for years, so why shouldn't I have something for myself for a change? Constantine might take issue with it, but if he did it wouldn't be because he wanted me in particular. I wasn't special to him. I was just a vessel. He hadn't even told the press that I'd been kidnapped, after all.

But I wasn't just a vessel to Val. And he wanted *me*, so why resist?

A night, I told myself. I'd let myself have a night where I was his and he was mine and we could have the passion we'd never had as children. Where kisses could become more and our games wouldn't be about pushing each other into the sea, but touching each other in bed.

I was allowed this. I was finally allowed to be with the boy I'd once loved and then lost.

'What happened to you after you left the beach?' I kept my voice very casual. It had been so many years ago that that particular pain had long since scabbed over. 'I found out you and Constantine had gone back to Madrid and I thought you'd contact me. But you didn't. I didn't hear anything.'

Valentin's eyes glittered strangely in the light and I saw something dark cross his face. I could also feel his body tense beneath me. This wasn't something he wanted to talk about, was it?

'Well,' he said softly. 'That's quite the story. Are you sure you want to hear it?'

A chill whispered over my skin. It was going to be something awful, wasn't it? Something to do with his father, Domingo, the psychopath.

I stared into Valentin's eyes, the chill settling deeper into my soul. I hadn't fully taken on board what he'd said about his father before, but that soft note in his voice and that glitter in his eyes…

What had his childhood *really* been like?

I'd never thought about it as a kid, not in any depth. We'd complained to each other about our parents, of course, but that was what kids did. All parents were mean and unfair. But Domingo…

'Tell me,' I said, staring into those mesmerising eyes. 'I want to know.'

'Don't say I didn't warn you.' Valentin didn't let my hair go, rubbing a lock of it between his thumb and forefinger. 'Domingo didn't want me seeing you, as you already know. But naturally I ignored him, because I always ignored him. He wouldn't have found out that I was still meeting with you if Constantine hadn't told him.'

A shock went through me. 'Constantine told him?'

Valentin lifted a shoulder. 'Oh, yes. He was such a good little soldier.'

'But…he's your brother.' I didn't want to believe Constantine could have done something like that, yet deep down I knew that of course he would have. He was such a stickler for rules.

'I tried to protect him by drawing Domingo's attention as much as possible so he would leave Constantine alone,' Valentin said. 'I…didn't know Domingo had been manipulating him behind my back and turning him against me. Not until he told Domingo about us.' Something in his handsome face shifted. 'That's when I knew I'd failed. That Domingo had got to him.'

Shock rippled through me. 'What do you mean, you failed? Why?'

'You have to understand,' Valentin said, his attention on the lock of my hair. 'Psychopaths don't need a reason to do what they do. They manipulate to get what they want for their own amusement. Because they like it. And I can't blame Constantine for choosing Domingo over me. We weren't allowed friends. Not even pets. Domingo didn't want us to form any emotional attachments to anything or anyone except him, and he didn't like it that Constantine and I were close. And I had no time for Constantine. I was too obsessed with you.'

His gaze came back to mine. 'Seeing you, meeting you, was like coming across an oasis in the desert, or a spot of colour in a black-and-white world. You were special, Olivia.'

I couldn't take it in. No friends? No pets? No emotional attachments? No wonder Constantine was so cold and so detached.

'I should have spent more time with Constantine,' Val went on, 'but I didn't, and that's my failure. Perhaps, if I had, he wouldn't have turned into Domingo. Anyway, that's all water under the bridge now. He found out I was still seeing you and told Domingo, and we were shipped back to Spain the next day. Then he took away my phone and my computer and he locked me in a room in the basement of our house in Madrid. I wasn't allowed to see anyone or speak to anyone.'

I didn't know what to say. He hadn't been able to contact me even if he'd wanted to and it wasn't because he hadn't cared. It was because his father had taken him prisoner.

The sympathy I'd felt earlier tugged harder. Two boys' lives had been thoroughly blighted by the one person who was supposed to have protected them. Who'd abused and manipulated them instead, not to mention ruining the relationship between them, because that was obvious to me too.

'That's awful,' I said. Such a meaningless and trite statement. Yet what else could I say? It *was* awful.

Val's mouth curved in a bitter smile. 'Yes, it is, isn't it? Domingo was quite subtle. He knew a beating wouldn't do anything, since I didn't care about pain. But he knew how to hurt me in other ways.' That bitter smile deepened. 'He told me he'd keep me there for as long as it took for me to learn how to obey.'

A cold feeling began to wrap itself around my heart. 'So…how long did he keep you there for?'

Val's expression didn't flicker. 'Six months.'

The cold feeling pulled tight, making it difficult to breathe.

Six months. He'd been kept a prisoner for six months.

I'd cried and cried when I'd never heard from him. And then I'd got angry. I'd hated him for a time, thinking he'd lied when he'd told me he loved me. That everything about our relationship had been a lie. He didn't love me, and he didn't care about me. And all I was was just a silly teenage girl who'd fallen for a handsome boy who'd lied to her for fun.

But he hadn't lied.

He'd been a prisoner.

'Val…' My heart felt strangely tight. 'I…'

'I don't need your pity, little star.' His voice was so mild. 'Domingo wanted to teach me a lesson and so he did. I could have promised to obey him, and he might have let me out, but I was still trying to protect Constantine.'

My heart tightened even further. 'You remained a prisoner for six months to protect your brother? After he told on you? On us?'

'Yes.' There was a bitter humour in his eyes. 'It wasn't his fault he turned out the way he did. I should have been there for him, and I wasn't.'

'Oh, Val.'

'I'd probably still be there if someone hadn't slipped me the key to the door and I was able to get out. Do you know, there were no windows? And once a week Domingo would take me outside to show me everything I was missing.' Val's gaze turned distant. 'He hated that I wouldn't give in. It made him so furious. He left me there three weeks once. I thought I was going to go mad...'

Horror gripped me, along with an aching pity that, no matter how hard I tried not to feel it, threaded through me all the same. Because behind his smile I could see that the boy had started to die even before that accident. He'd been so full of life, burning bright... What must being trapped in a room for six months have done to him? Not being able to see the sun, or the stars. The moon... Not being able to feel the air on his face or hear the sound of the sea...

And you hating him because he didn't text you.

He frowned suddenly, his gaze sharpening. 'Don't, Livvy. Whatever you're thinking, don't.'

But he'd given me some honesty and so I had to give him some in return.

'I was very angry with you after you left,' I said. 'For not saying goodbye. And then you didn't contact me. I didn't get a text or an email or a call. I thought... I thought you'd forgotten me.'

He opened his mouth, but I laid a finger across his lips. 'Then you died. And I was angry about that. I was angry with you for a very long time.'

His mouth moved again, but I pressed my finger slightly harder, feeling the softness of his lips against my skin. The only thing about him that was soft. 'I'm sorry I didn't know the truth. I'm sorry that I never asked you what Domingo was really like or…or what kind of life you had.' And I was so sorry. More than he'd ever guess. 'I probably should have picked it up or…'

He pulled my finger away, holding on to my hand. 'No, you don't need to be sorry. You were only fifteen and you had your own issues to deal with. You weren't to know what Domingo was like. And I didn't tell you, not the extent of it.'

'But I—'

'I didn't want you to know. I didn't want you to worry. Because there was nothing you could have done.' He gathered my fingers in his and kissed the tips of them the way he'd used to. 'Domingo had too much power, and you were only a kid, and so was I.' He let out a breath, an emotion I couldn't quite read flickering over his face. 'I wish I could have done more, but it's too late for that now.'

Was that regret? I couldn't be sure. Whatever it was, my heart ached for him and what he'd had to put up with. What he'd had to endure, he and Constantine both.

Domingo made my father look like father of the year.

'Anyway,' Valentin went on, brushing his mouth over my fingertips again. 'Enough about me. What about you? What happened to turn my Livvy into such a formidable CEO?'

Formidable. Yes, I was. Because that was what I'd wanted to be. That's where I'd put my effort. I'd become a diamond that wouldn't shatter, crack or get scratched. I was impervious.

Are you, though? Sitting naked in his lap in a silly dress, allowing him to kiss your fingers like you're a princess? You know what the next step is.

No, of course that wouldn't be the next step. There was a vast gap between choosing to sit in a man's lap and staying in a loveless marriage while putting up with all kinds of emotional cruelty.

'Well, after you died, I needed something to fill my time.' My voice sounded cool even though I hadn't meant it to. 'And I know that back then I always said I didn't want to run Wintergreen, but I changed my mind. So I studied hard at school and then went to university. And, when I asked Dad to take me on, he didn't refuse.'

Valentin's black eyes watched me with his usual intense focus. 'Is that what this is?'

'This?' I frowned. 'What do you mean?'

He touched my cheek, his fingers feathering over my skin before falling down to my shoulder and brushing gently along it. 'This tension. This…toughness. You're all bright and shiny and hard, like a diamond.'

I should have been pleased that he'd noticed. Pleased that he'd accurately guessed what I'd become. But for some reason it didn't feel like he was complimenting me.

'You say that like it's a bad thing.' I forced away the shiver at his touch. 'Hardness is always admired in men, but it's never admired in women.'

'That's true. And, to be clear, I don't think it's an inherently bad thing. You need a certain hardness when it comes to business. But when it doesn't come naturally to someone, they over-compensate. They become hard all the way through. All their passion is leached away, which is a pity, because good business needs passion too.'

A thread of annoyance wound through me. 'I'm not over-compensating, if that's what you're suggesting.'

A smile flickered around his mouth and it wasn't the same bitter one I'd seen before. This was more rueful, and somehow a hundred times more attractive. 'Actually, I was suggesting that.' He touched my cheek again, his fingertips tracing the line of my jaw. 'You never used to be like this, not so hard and bright and shiny. Why? What's the purpose of it? It's brittle, and I don't think you like it. I think it's hard work for you.' His smile deepened. 'You're much more yourself when you're slapping my face and pushing me off the jetty into the sea.'

The annoyance was starting to become anger now, and I could feel myself freezing over, trying to shut it out. Trying to detach myself from the emotion.

How he always managed to get under my guard, I didn't know, but it wasn't what I wanted. Not while I was naked and lying in his arms.

'Yes, well, I shouldn't have done any of those things,' I said coolly. 'And you're not wrong about me being a diamond. Diamonds are created under pressure, and they're impervious. Which is the best way to be when it comes to managing my company.'

I shifted in his lap, deciding I needed to get off him. It had been nice while it lasted, but I wasn't a pet. I wasn't going to stay there.

But his hands dropped suddenly to my hips, gripping me, preventing me from moving. 'Why?' he demanded. 'Who told you that?'

'My father. And he wasn't wrong.'

'Yes, well, your father is dead.' Valentin wasn't smiling now and there was something fierce glittering in his eyes. 'And he can't see you here. There's only me and I don't care how impervious you are. You don't need to guard yourself with me.'

'Don't I?' I shot back before I could stop myself. 'When you're manipulating me at every step, with my favourite foods and wine, and talking about the past? Reminding me every minute of that girl I used to be? You told me yourself that you're going to make me fall in love with you, and that's exactly what you're trying to do, isn't it?'

His expression hardened, his grip not easing one iota. 'Yes.'

It was clear he did not like having to admit that, yet he had, and it made my anger at him ease a fraction. But only a fraction.

'Well, then,' I said. 'I shouldn't need to explain why relaxing my guard with you will never be an option.'

A muscle flicked in his jaw, and he was silent a long moment. Then he said, 'There's a reason I call you "little star". Did you know that? It's because that's what you are. You're not a diamond, Olivia Wintergreen. You're a star. And stars are made to burn.'

And you're still burning all these years later. Burning for him.

No, I wasn't. I'd killed that fire stone-dead and it would never burn again.

'Let me go,' I said, pushing at his chest.

His fingers tightened a moment, his gaze getting hot. 'Are you sure?'

And I could feel it again, the wild chemistry that seemed to have got even more intense now we'd slept together building between us. The hunger gathering inside me despite all the barriers I'd tried to put between myself and it.

Because, no, I wasn't sure.

There was a part of me that didn't want him to let me go. That wanted him to hold me tight and keep me close. The part of me that wanted to know more about the man he'd become—a difficult, dangerous, challenging yet fascinating man.

The part of me that wanted to burn.

But I wasn't going to. He was too tempting, and already I'd forgotten myself enough to surrender to him on the sand. To let him wash me, feed me and hold me in his lap as if I were a child.

I'd had my night of pleasure and it was over now.

'Yes,' I said flatly. 'I'm sure.'

Something flickered in his night-black gaze

and for a second I thought he wouldn't do it. But then his fingers released me and I slid off his lap.

'What changed?' he asked, an edge to his voice. 'What did you do with my Livvy?'

'I'm not your Livvy, Valentin.' I turned back towards the villa. 'And nothing's changed. It was nice to reconnect, but I have a company to run and a fiancé to get back to.'

'What? Did you think I was joking?' His voice was low and somehow menacing. 'Did you think that sex was all I wanted? That we could sleep together, have dinner and then I'd fly you back home tomorrow?'

I stopped dead, a shudder going through me.

Yes, of course I'd thought that. Perhaps not consciously, but I'd assumed…

He's not that boy, remember? And he's dangerous.

But I wasn't that girl, either, and perhaps I, too, was dangerous.

I turned around, the silk of my tunic brushing over my skin, making me very aware all of a sudden of how I was naked beneath it.

Val had risen to his feet, the rueful, beautiful smile vanishing as if it had never been there. His handsome face had gone hard, a razor's edge in his black eyes. He still burned—he'd never been cold like Constantine—but this fire was fierce and it was hungry. Like it had been back in the ballroom of the Silvera mansion.

I'd never been more aware that this was the man he was now. That the past fifteen years of his life had clearly been a furnace, tempering him. He was not a man who could be crossed. It was clear he did not like the word 'no'.

'Then I'll damn well learn to fly and take the plane,' I said, throwing down the gauntlet, because I wasn't a woman who liked hearing the word no. 'I'm not your prisoner, Val. And I won't be told what to do—not by you, not by anyone.

'You're not marrying him. I won't let you.'

'Really? And how are you going to stop me?' I lifted a brow. 'Or are you going to lock me in, the way your father did to you?'

'He's *not* my father,' Valentin spat all of a sudden. 'And I don't need to lock you in.' He began to come towards me, striding down the jetty with all that predatory grace; all bright, fierce beauty. Lucifer, the light bringer.

Perhaps I should have run. But I hadn't run earlier, and I wasn't going to do that now. Besides, he wasn't going to hurt me. He was only going to intimidate me into doing what he wanted and, well, he could try.

So I stood my ground, lifting my chin. Letting him see he couldn't cow me or frighten me into doing his bidding.

He stopped, barely inches away, surrounding me with the seductive heat of his body and scent of cinnamon and salt. Reminding me that he was all man, and that I was all woman, and that I wanted him. No matter what I told myself about distance, I wanted him.

He said nothing, reaching out and taking the front of my silk tunic between his hands and jerking it apart. The silk tore soundlessly, the halves falling open, leaving me naked.

Heat and desire burned hot in his eyes as his gaze raked over me, and I didn't flinch from it. I let him look. Because it came to me that I had a power I hadn't fully understood until now. A uniquely feminine power that I'd always underestimated and dismissed.

The power of sex.

He wanted me. But he couldn't have me unless I let him.

He reached for me.

'Don't touch me.' I held his gaze, letting him see that I wasn't going to give in; giving him a taste of his own medicine.

His hands stopped where they were, halfway to reaching for my hips. Fury lit in his eyes as I saw him battle with his better self.

'What is this?' he growled. 'A test?'

'No. It's an ultimatum. If you want me again, you have to promise to let me go. And then you'll fly me back to London so I can marry Constantine.'

He cursed under his breath, something harsh in Spanish. 'You should know that I do not take kindly to ultimatums.'

'Too bad, because that's what you're getting.'

His eye gleamed like a furnace. 'It never worked for Domingo. Why would it work for you?'

'Because I am not Domingo.' I reached out and placed my palm against his rock-hard chest, tempting fate. Tempting him. 'Enjoy your cold bed.'

Then I turned on my heel and walked back naked to the villa.

CHAPTER TWELVE

Valentin

I SAT ON the jetty all night, gritting my teeth and seething. Fighting my rage.

Towards dawn, I flung myself into the sea to get rid of the heat burning ferociously inside me and then stalked back to the villa.

I went to my bedroom. The bed sheets were still rumpled from making love to Olivia. I could still smell her on the air, sweetness and feminine musk. It made me even harder than I already was, which didn't help my temper.

I dumped my clothes and then went into the shower, turned it to cold and stood under the water, letting it fall like needles of ice on my hot skin.

She'd been so very beautiful standing there on the jetty the night before, unflinching as I'd torn the silk of her tunic apart. She'd stood her

ground, naked and proud, like a goddess made
of starlight.

Telling me, no. Telling me that, if I wanted
her, I'd have to let her go.

No one told me to do anything. No one. Not
since Domingo.

How could I let her go, anyway? Let her go
and marry another man? A man I'd done my
best to protect.

My brother. My twin.

I'd wanted to ignore her, to grab her, to show
her how easily her will could be broken with
just the touch of my hand. I could have had her
on the jetty, gasping and begging for me. I could
have had her warm and wet and willing. I could
have made her forget all about that stupid ultimatum of hers.

But I couldn't stop thinking about what she'd
flung at me—about how she couldn't let down
her guard with me—because I'd been manipulating her ever since we'd got here. And I hadn't
been able to take that last step. A boundary had
sprung up inside me and I hadn't realised I had
it.

She'd said not to touch her, and I couldn't.
Just as I couldn't ignore what she'd said about
using her favourite foods and those memories
of our childhood to manipulate her.

I hadn't thought about it at the time. I'd just

done what I'd had to do to get what I wanted. And, yes, looking at it like that, I *had* manipulated her. I'd wanted her to remember what we'd had as children, what we'd been to each other… Yet, as she kept saying to me, she wasn't that child any longer. And neither was I.

So, I couldn't touch her. And I couldn't use food, memories or even sex to make her change her mind.

Fundamentally, I couldn't ignore her choice, because wasn't that what Domingo had taken from me? Hadn't that been my whole childhood?

Yet wasn't that what you were doing all along? Making your own choices anyway just to spite him? To show him he couldn't beat you, that he couldn't win?

No, it had had never been about winning. It had been about protecting Constantine. That had always been the goal.

Yes, and you failed.

I pushed the thought away, not wanting to dwell on it. This wasn't about Domingo and Constantine, anyway. This was about Olivia. And, no matter what she said, no matter what ultimatums she'd flung at me, I still wasn't going to let her go back to Madrid to marry my psychopathic brother, and that was final.

After my shower, I stalked down the wide

wooden hallway and into the room I used as an office. Like the rest of the villa, it had large windows and big sliding glass doors that led out onto the deck that surrounded the house.

The island and the villa I'd built was my favourite place to be. There was nothing shut-in about it, nothing hemmed in. Everywhere there were views of the ocean, and all you needed to do to get out was to slide back one of those big glass doors.

It was a hangover of being shut in that basement room for months. I still didn't like being confined and, once I'd had money, I'd spent it on wide vistas and freedom.

The room had bookshelves lining the walls, full of books in a wide array of different subjects and genres, and anything else that took my interest. A large, smooth white stone. An intricate shell. A piece of driftwood in an interesting shape. A piece of coral, bleached white, that had washed up on the beach.

I liked that I could put whatever I wanted on the shelves. I liked that I could do whatever I wanted with the villa. After a childhood such as mine, where everything had been tightly controlled, being able to make such small choices was a luxury I still enjoyed, no matter how many years had gone by.

A large wooden desk with clean lines stood

near one of the windows, a wafer-thin computer screen sitting on top of it. I went over to the desk and sat down, turning on my computer.

I wanted to check in with my lawyers, as well as catch up on the media to see what progress—if any—had been made with my brother. I hadn't had any alerts overnight, which meant he hadn't made any move, which I thought was odd.

Surely, he wouldn't just let me walk away with Olivia? Especially when she seemed so keen to get back to him. Domingo wouldn't have permitted it, that was for sure.

I leaned back in my chair, scrolling through the day's news, most of my brain occupied with what my next move was going to be. I had to stop Olivia being so suspicious of me, get her to trust me somehow, and that meant changing my methods.

I couldn't let her leave, but perhaps I could let her lead our interactions. That wouldn't be manipulating her, not if she took the initiative. Perhaps she could tell me more about her company and her plans for it. I already knew a lot about it, but not all. And, if sex was out, fine. I didn't need it that badly. Maybe it would give me the chance to learn more about Olivia the woman rather than Olivia the girl.

After all, she hadn't seemed to dislike my

company. I'd told her about Domingo, about what had happened all those years ago, and she'd told me how angry she'd been with me for not contacting her. Which I completely understood.

Your fault, though. You could have given in.

I sneered at the thought. Given in? To Domingo? And let him turn his sights on Constantine? Never.

Constantine had sat outside the basement door even though he'd been forbidden to go near it, breaking the rules for me so he could slip notes underneath it. Notes asking me why I wouldn't just give in, because Papa wouldn't let me out until I did. Papa would keep me there for ever.

There'd been no apology from him, though. No apology for condemning me to months in a windowless room with no sky, glimpse of the stars or a laughing girl to keep me company.

No apology, even though I'd been making myself the target of Domingo's attentions for years for *him*.

I hadn't been angry about it. Because that had been the moment I'd understood that he wasn't my twin any more. He wasn't even my brother. He was Domingo's son in every way, and that was why there'd been no apology. He didn't care about me. He didn't care about Olivia. And why would he? Psychopaths had no empathy.

Anger collected inside me along with a bitter grief that still hurt even after all these years. Fury at Domingo and what he'd done to Constantine, what he'd done to us both and the bond that used to exist between us. The bond he'd broken, leaving me with no choice but to take from Constantine his company and his power so he wouldn't hurt anyone the way Domingo had.

Fury at myself for failing him.

I growled and reached out abruptly, sweeping the offending computer monitor off the desk and onto the floor. It cracked satisfyingly, but I was still furious. Domingo was dead; I couldn't take my rage out on him, but I had to get rid of it somehow. Yet the only options here were exercise or sex. And, since sex was clearly off the table, exercise it would have to be.

The gym was down the other end of the villa and after I'd changed into my workout gear I got on the treadmill and put myself through a punishing run.

Olivia wouldn't like me keeping her here, but letting her leave wasn't an option. I had to protect her. I'd failed my brother, but I wouldn't fail her.

She could deny me her body, but that was fine. I could outlast her. We'd soon see who was

more resolute. I'd been beaten, starved and isolated. I'd been locked in a windowless room for
six months because I'd refused to surrender. I'd
died and built an empire from nothing at all on
the strength of my will alone.

Domingo himself hadn't been able to win
against me and neither would she.

And where will that get you?

The thought came out of nowhere, whispering through my brain like a snake in the grass.
I ran harder, trying to leave it behind, because
it was a stupid question.

What would it get me? It would get me her.
In the end, she would be mine.

*And did resisting Domingo ever get you what
you wanted? Even once?*

I growled again, gritting my teeth as I hit
the incline button, tilting the treadmill up to its
maximum and running even harder.

Of course it had worked with Domingo. He'd
done exactly what I'd wanted him to, which was
turn his attention on me. My rebellions had kept
him busy while he'd left Constantine alone.
Constantine had been the good boy, doing everything Domingo had said, while I'd made sure
I was the bad one. The one who disobeyed, the
one he tried to punish.

But I never gave in. Not once.

You died. You lost everything. Your brother

became Domingo and you broke Olivia's heart. How is that winning?

I gave a guttural roar, slapping the stop button and standing on the treadmill, panting, sweat streaming down my body. Because, as much as I didn't want that thought in my head, it wound its way through my brain all the same.

It was true. That last burst of defiance hadn't worked as well as it should have. It had ended up with me 'dying', and it had ended up hurting Olivia.

She'd thought I didn't care about her; that I hadn't called her because I'd forgotten about her.

She didn't matter as much as your need to win against Domingo.

I tried to shove that thought away, going over to the gym door that led to the deck and stepping outside. Stripping off my sweaty clothes, I dove head-first into the water straight from the deck, letting the sea wash away the sweat.

But I couldn't get that thought out of my head.

What if I'd given in and agreed to never see her again? He would have left her alone because she'd never interested him. She was only a tool he'd used to get to me.

Perhaps if I'd done what he'd asked, perhaps if I'd made that promise, I could have found some way to get a message to her without Domingo finding out, to let her know what had happened. Then, when I'd finally grown up and Domingo had no power over me any longer, I could have come for her.

Perhaps if I'd done that we could have been married now.

And she might not have turned herself into that hard, cold diamond. She might have waited for you. But you failed her, like you failed your brother.

Something hot twisted in my chest, but I shoved it away. I couldn't go down that route; there was no point. The past was fixed. I couldn't change it. But I could certainly make things better for the future, so I would.

Surfacing, I turned in the direction of the villa and swam slowly back to the steps that led back up to the deck, turning an idea over in my head.

Compromise had always been difficult for me, but I had to give Olivia something. A gesture of good faith. A counter-offer. Something that would get us what we both wanted but would still ensure she didn't marry Constantine. Because, his psychopathic tendencies aside, she didn't really want him.

But she did want me. And I had everything he did, plus something else: the ability to give her pleasure. After all, it hadn't been his name she'd called out under the stars last night, and it hadn't been him she'd been thinking of.

It was me. All me.

Once I was out of the water, I grabbed a towel, dried myself and got changed. Then I strode down the wide hallway again to the guest bedroom Olivia was in.

The door was closed and, even though I was tempted to just walk in, I didn't. I raised a hand and knocked. Politely. Like a gentleman. Because if I was going to win her I needed to at least stop paying lip service to the idea and actually start acting like one.

'Come in,' Olivia called.

I pushed the door open and strode in.

And stopped dead in the middle of the room.

Olivia was sunbathing on the lounger on the deck just outside her room.

And she was naked.

CHAPTER THIRTEEN

Olivia

NAKED SUNBATHING WAS a calculated gamble. But, if Valentin could climb out of the ocean stark naked and wander about in front of me, I could certainly lie on the sun-lounger without any clothes on in front of him.

And I'd had to do something. I couldn't sit in my room, twiddling my thumbs all day. I'd had to act.

This morning I'd already been in touch with Rachel, making enquiries as to flights from the Maldives. She was surprised that I wanted to come home so soon but hadn't questioned it.

I couldn't let anyone know the real situation, because that was my only advantage. If the board didn't know I'd been kidnapped by Constantine's twin brother, if they still thought I was on some Caribbean holiday with Constantine himself, then at least I wouldn't look weak.

I wouldn't look like some damn trophy wife two brothers were fighting over.

Which is what you are.

Not for much longer. Not if I could help it.

I had to get back to Madrid, and quickly, and I'd use every weapon in my arsenal to do so, including my new-found feminine power: sex.

It was the kind of tactic my mother had often used, prettying herself up for Dad with a nice dress, salon hair and expert make-up. Sometimes it had worked and sometimes it hadn't, and I'd never known why she'd bothered. Why she hadn't just up and left him, because I certainly would have.

Using such tactics myself felt like a step in the wrong direction, but Val was so strong-willed. So stubborn. Yet I knew he had one weakness: me.

I'd heard him come striding down the hallway and it had been a matter of moments to pull off the bikini I'd been wearing in preparation for a swim and lie down on the lounger, my heart beating fast.

I had to make him want me more than he wanted to keep me prisoner. Show him what he could have if he gave me what I wanted.

But you're using the same tactics against him that Domingo used.

The thought sat uneasily in my head, memories of what he'd told me last night replaying themselves over and over. Of him locked in that room. Of him wanting to draw his father's attention to save his brother. Of the anger inside him whenever he talked about it that he probably thought he'd hidden. But he couldn't hide it from me. I could see the flames in his eyes.

No wonder he'd always burned so brightly. He was a furnace of rage.

A part of me wanted to help him, while another part wanted to get away from him as quickly as possible. Because I knew what happened to women who stayed with difficult men. Their lives became miserable.

My mother's being a case in point. She'd stayed true to a man who'd married her because she'd been young and beautiful. A man who hadn't respected her, who hadn't even seemed to love her. Who'd blamed her for something that hadn't even been her fault.

So, if I stayed with Val, what would happen to me?

He'd burn you both alive...

My thoughts fractured as I heard his step and I threw one arm over my eyes, even though the sun umbrella was providing me with shade. I didn't want to see him just yet, not until my armour was in place.

His footsteps came to a complete stop.

Good. He'd obviously seen me.

I kept my arm over my eyes, my heart racing despite all my efforts to still it.

The room was silent, but I could sense his presence. He was watching me. I could feel the pressure of his gaze sending hot shivers all over my bare skin.

I'd never realised before how erotic it was to lie there naked while a man looked at every part of me. Wanting me. And he wanted me; I knew he did.

I didn't move. Every sense I had was trained on him, so very conscious of my nakedness and the ache between my thighs, a growing neediness that was difficult to ignore.

'Nice to see you enjoying the sun.' The deep, rough sound of his voice came from very near. 'I hope you've got some sunscreen on.'

He must be standing right beside my lounger.

I kept my arm where it was, my heart pounding, my mouth dry. Then I gave a stretch, arching my back as if I'd been sleepy and was trying to wake up.

'I do,' I murmured. 'But it's probably worn off now.' I paused. 'You could put some on me, if you like.'

He laughed, the sound genuine and deeply sensual, making me want to say something else to get him to do it again. 'For an inexperienced virgin, you certainly know how to play the seduction game. I'm impressed, Livvy.' I heard him move and then I could smell his aftershave—cinnamon and masculine musk. Delicious.

The squab on the lounger tilted slightly as I felt him sit on the end of it.

Why was he here? Was this a concession? Had I won?

You don't want to win; not this game.

Maybe not. But I was tired of him holding all the cards. I wanted some of my own.

I shifted my arm at last.

Val was sitting on the end of the lounger, the bottle of sunscreen in one hand. He was in a black T-shirt today, and worn jeans, and he looked just as delicious as he had the day before. His expression was hungry and he made no effort to hide the desire in his gaze as he swept it down my body, lingering on my breasts and then further down between my legs.

Abruptly, my mouth was as dry as that sandy beach, and it came to me that this little plan had the potential to backfire. I hadn't realised that in tempting him I could just as easily end up tempting myself.

He lifted the bottle and squeezed some sunscreen into his hand. 'Turn over, little star. Let me put some of this on your back.' One black brow lifted. 'Unless you'd like me to start with your front?'

I should tell him not to touch me, to leave—or, better yet, make him watch me as I put sunscreen on myself. But everything in me was aching for his touch and I couldn't resist it. And why not, when I enjoyed him touching me?

After all, it wasn't as if I was going to let him do anything more.

I said nothing, rolling over onto my front.

He shifted and I felt him ease aside my hair so it fell over my shoulder, the strands silky and soft against my skin. He moved closer on the edge of the lounger, the denim of his jeans brushing against my bare hip. The heat of his body was so very near, the familiar warm scent of him making me dizzy.

Are you sure lying here naked was a good idea?

It had been at the time. Now, I wasn't so sure. All I could think about was why I'd thought surrendering to him had been so very bad. It hadn't been last night; no, it had been…good. *So* good. Perhaps I didn't need to get back to Constantine so quickly. He didn't seem to be looking for me, after all, and a couple more days with Val surely wouldn't hurt…

And then what? You might not want to leave. You might want to stay here for ever and marry him, the way he told you that you would. You'll end up giving him everything he wants, become his perfect trophy wife the way your mother was...

No. No, I was *not* going to let that happen. I was stronger than that and certainly stronger than my mother. She hadn't been a diamond. She'd been nothing but marshmallow melting in my father's hand.

I was different. I wouldn't allow myself to be any man's toy or trophy, and especially not for the sake of a little hot sex.

The only things I needed from a man were Constantine's money and his genetic material, and that was all. Anything else, I'd get myself.

Cool liquid trickled down my spine and then Val's hands were on me, warm and strong and gentle, moving with long, sensual strokes as he massaged in the sunscreen.

Oh, he was so good at that. My whole body clenched tight with desire, both relaxing and thrilling at the same time, which didn't make any sense, yet was obviously happening. I wanted to melt into the lounger, or turn over and arch my back, encourage him to touch my hardening nipples and then go lower to touch other more sensitive, more desperate parts of me.

But, no, I had to stay strong.

'So,' he murmured, his voice like liquid

honey. 'What's so very important about marrying Constantine?'

I had my head pillowed on my forearm, trying to pay attention to what he was saying and not the caress of his stroking hands. 'Dad made some…unfortunate business decisions in the last years of his life and it left the company in a financial hole. So when Constantine offered his help, I accepted.'

'He offered?'

'Yes. He'd heard we were in difficulty and came to me with a proposal.'

'Marriage was part of the proposal?'

There didn't seem to be any reason not to tell him.

'Yes.'

'How very medieval of him.' Val massaged my shoulders deliciously, then stroked down the length of my spine. 'I didn't think he was the marrying type.'

I stared into the darkness behind my closed lids, remembering how he'd come to me. And even though I'd prepared myself the shock of seeing him again after all those years had still stolen my breath away. He'd come into my office and for a second all I'd been able to think was, *Val. It's Val.* And then reality had asserted itself and, quite unexpectedly, I'd almost burst into tears.

'He thought it would be beneficial for both of us,' I said, forcing the memory away. 'He said it was time he settled down and got married. Produced some heirs.'

Val's hands paused. Then I felt more cool liquid on my hot skin as he began to smooth it lower over the curve of one buttock.

I shivered, fighting the urge to lift my hips and press into his hand.

'Ah.' His voice was utterly neutral. 'Was that a condition of his financial help?'

'Yes.'

Val stroked over my rear, cupping me gently. His fingers curled between my thighs just a little, the tips grazing lightly over my most sensitive flesh.

I bit my lip, struggling not to tremble in reaction.

'And I assume he won't just pay the debts?' Val went on, as if he wasn't playing havoc with my senses. 'He'll want some kind of financial control over the company for a time?'

Why was he asking me these questions? If he'd been watching me all this time, he must have some idea already of what Constantine had offered.

'Do you genuinely not know?' I tried to keep the huskiness from my voice. 'Or are you just trying to manipulate me again?'

He gave a low laugh. 'And you're not doing the same thing? Flaunting all this delicious nakedness at me?'

Strangely, that made me want to smile. He was teasing, yet it didn't feel as if it was at my expense this time, but his own. 'Perhaps,' I said. 'Is it working?'

'I couldn't possibly say.'

I felt him draw a small pattern at the small of my back and allowed myself the smile. Yes, it was working.

'Anyway,' he went on. 'Maybe I did know that's why Constantine was marrying you. I'd still like to know the details, though.'

I relaxed a little. 'He said he'd manage Wintergreen until the company was solvent. To instil confidence in my leadership, et cetera.'

Val had moved on to massaging sunscreen into my thighs and the backs of my knees, and his touch felt so good, I relaxed a little further.

'He'll never give it back to you,' Val said casually, as if it wasn't *my* company he was talking about. 'You know that, don't you?'

Ah, right. So we were back to Constantine being a psychopath, were we?

'No, I don't know that. Why would he keep it? He's got no reason to.'

'He'll want to retain something to hold over your head.' Val's hands moved down my calves, making me want to moan in pleasure. 'It was one of Domingo's favourite tactics and, like I told you, Constantine has become him.'

I didn't believe that for a second, but it was interesting that Val believed it so wholeheartedly.

'Why do you insist on thinking that?' I asked, biting back a sigh of contentment. 'Constantine is many things, but he's not Domingo.'

Val's stroking hands paused. 'He's charmed you already, I see.'

'Charm?' I didn't hold back my scorn. 'Constantine? Have you met him?'

There was a silence. Then Val said, 'Turn over for me, little star.'

I stayed where I was. 'Tell me why you're so wedded to this psychopath idea and I might.'

Another silence.

'He slipped me notes under the door.' Val sounded oddly muted. 'They were all, *"Why don't you do what Papa says?" "Give in and he'll let you out"*. There was no apology for betraying me. There was no empathy there at all. And you know what they say about psychopaths.'

I heard it then, the note of pain and fury. But I couldn't tell whether it was directed at Constantine, his father or at himself.

'Well?' he asked. 'Will you turn over for me?'

Not an order this time, but a request. And

why not? He'd given me a choice and, while his stroking hands might be a manipulation, it was one I'd engineered myself. And that we were both enjoying, apparently.

Besides, I liked his hands on me. It felt as if all my bones had melted.

I turned, keeping my eyes closed against the bright light, and I heard his soft intake of breath. It made me smile, even though I knew I shouldn't. 'It's still working, then?'

'You're enjoying this, aren't you? Minx. And, yes, it's still working.' The husky note of amusement lingered in his sexy voice. 'So he wants heirs, you said? Nothing wrong with being a wife and mother, but you must want more than that for yourself. You're ambitious and driven; I can see that. And I'd love to hear about your company and what your plans are for it.'

Despite myself, I couldn't help feeling a warm glow of pleasure at the genuine interest in his voice. Then cool liquid slid between my breasts and I shuddered as a different kind of pleasure, a more sensual kind, joined it.

'I want to make sure all the diamonds we sell and use in our jewellery are from ethical sources,' I said, because again there was no reason not to tell him and this was a pet project of mine. 'Because at the moment they're not.'

'Well, I approve whole-heartedly of that. Why isn't that the case already?'

'Because the board are dragging their feet. They're concerned about the bottom line.' And they were suspicious of me introducing new ideas that weren't in step with theirs. As if insisting people's lives were more important than money was a new idea.

'Sounds about right.' He stroked down over my chest, massaging in the sunscreen, his fingers curving around my breasts, his touch sensual yet not wholly sexual. 'And I'm not sure having Constantine in charge will help you with that.'

I bit my lip, giving up the fight to keep myself separate from the pleasure of his touch, relaxing entirely into it as his hands moved on, caressing my hips and down over my stomach.

'So, let me propose a counter-offer. You could marry me instead.' His fingers gently massaged the sensitive skin above my pubic bone, but no further. Not touching me where I so badly wanted him to. 'Marry me, and in return I'll pay Wintergreen's debts. I won't oversee your management. It's clear you have the skills to do it, and anyway the debts were your father's, not yours. You shouldn't have to pay for his mistakes.'

I stilled beneath his hands, oddly taken off-guard by his insight. Was that why I'd felt uncomfortable with Constantine's offer? Because I had, though I could never really pinpoint why. But maybe it was simply that, in insisting on having financial oversight, he'd made me feel as if those debts were mine. As if I was responsible for the company's mismanagement, not Dad.

Val's fingers were on my thighs now, massaging in firm, sure strokes. 'I will give you freedom, Livvy,' he went on. 'I'll never tie you down or limit you. I'll take care of you when you want it. And I'll certainly give you as much pleasure as you can handle. I'll always satisfy you. I'll never leave you hungry.'

My brain struggled to process what he was saying, everything in me having melted completely into the sun-lounger.

It sounded good, I had to admit. Marry him instead, have Wintergreen's debts paid, be in control of the company. Have my freedom, though why he thought freedom was his to give was anyone's guess. But…he hadn't mentioned children.

He gave me one last stroke and then I felt him move away.

I took my forearm from my eyes, blinking against the sudden, painfully bright light.

Val stood next to the lounger, looking down at me, and I could see the hunger blazing in his eyes. His whole body radiated tension; he was holding himself back, but only barely.

You've done that to him. You've brought him to the edge.

'Well?' he demanded, suddenly fierce. 'What do you say?'

'What about an heir?' I asked, my voice thick and sleepy sounding. 'Constantine promised me that too.'

For the first time since he'd brought me here, I saw uncertainty ripple over his features. 'Children? Really?'

'Yes. Wintergreen is a family company and I need a family to pass it on to.'

All the warmth and desire in his eyes drained away, his expression shutting down hard. 'No,' he said flatly. 'No. I won't give you that.'

Something in my stomach lurched, even though I knew I should have expected it. After that night in the sea, I knew how he felt about the issue of kids.

But Wintergreen was important to me. Passing it on to my children was important to me. I'd hoped that by having Constantine I could bypass the issue of IVF, but if Val wasn't prepared to give me a child, then what else could I do?

'I'll have to give myself a child, then, won't I?' I said, holding his gaze. 'I assume that won't be a problem?'

He stared at me a long moment, emotions I didn't understand flickering in his black eyes, a muscle leaping in his strong jaw.

Then he carefully put down the bottle of sunscreen and, without a word, turned on his heel and walked out.

CHAPTER FOURTEEN

Valentin

A CHILD. SHE REALLY wanted a child.

I sat in my office, trying to work yet finding myself staring sightlessly at the computer screen once again.

I hadn't expected her to be so certain about it, though on reflection maybe I should have. As I'd already discovered, she was driven and ambitious, and Wintergreen was important to her. She'd worked hard to get where she was now and, as she'd told me, it was a family company and she needed a child to pass it on to, as her father had passed it on to her.

All of that was very logical.

The thought of children was…difficult. My genes were tainted through and through, and as for being a father…impossible. I couldn't be any kind of parent, not when I didn't know the first thing about being a good father. After all, it wasn't as if I'd had any good role models.

Still, I shouldn't have had a problem with her 'giving' herself a child, which I assumed meant IVF. Except I did have a problem. The moment she'd mentioned it, something inside me had twisted hard in denial. Almost as if I'd wanted her to have *my* child which, naturally, I didn't.

I shouldn't have walked out on her, though. I should have agreed and then put the sunscreen away and done what I'd been wanting to do ever since I'd seen her lying naked on the sun-lounger: celebrated our agreement by making her scream with pleasure.

But I hadn't.

I swivelled my chair round to look out of the window, where a glorious sunset was happening outside. However, I didn't see the colours. All I could see was her grey eyes, full of heat from my touch and yet equally full of steel.

She'd grown formidable, my Olivia. And we were at an impasse.

The same kind of impasse you had with Domingo.

A strange dread sat in my gut, along with a hot thread of anger.

This wasn't how I'd thought it would go. I'd thought that eventually, once she'd got over her anger at me for my supposed death, she'd re-

member what we had and fall into my arms. I'd
thought a week, tops.

A week hadn't passed yet, but nothing was
proceeding as I'd planned, and I was now in
uncharted territory.

Did you really think it would be that easy?

The dread grew stronger. I didn't want to
compromise, I didn't want to give in. My will
had had to be diamond-hard in order to combat
Domingo's, and I found it was difficult when
anyone went against it.

*But she's a diamond too. And one of you has
to make the first move.*

It was true. I'd seduced the girl, but it was the
woman who was in charge. And all the qualities
I'd seen in her all those years ago—the courage, strength and stubbornness—had crystal-
lised and hardened into that veneer.

She wasn't ripping off that veneer for me,
though. Every time I thought I was getting close
to her, down it would come.

I stared at the sunset flaming in the sky, my
thoughts ticking over.

How could I get beneath it? How could I
reach the heart of her?

Why do you want to so badly?

Because I loved her, of course. Why else?
And I wanted her to love me. But until she low-
ered her guard that wasn't going to happen. I

wanted her passion *and* her heart, yet I wasn't quite sure how to get them.

As I'd already thought, she didn't trust me. And letting her take the initiative today had only resulted in yet another business proposition. But I didn't want a business proposition, I realised. I didn't want her to marry me because I was going to pay her debts and give her a child.

I wanted her to marry me because she loved me, and that had *always* been my goal.

Which meant I needed to get serious about this.

The key to her love was her trust and, in order to get that, I would have to make the first move. I would have to show myself worthy.

But I couldn't be rash about it. I needed some time to think.

In the end, I gave us both a couple of days' break, letting the idea sit in the back of my head as I busied myself with other things. My brother, in other words.

I'd had no luck getting any kind of response from his lawyers and now he'd apparently gone to ground completely. It was frustrating, but it wasn't as if I didn't have anything else to do.

Lately, I'd been toying with the idea of venture capital. I liked new ideas, I found them exciting, and I had plenty of money to invest, and it seemed like an excellent new field to branch out into.

So, I occupied myself with that as well as keeping an eye on the media. There was still no mention of my reappearance, which meant Constantine had well and truly suppressed it, and I was curious about that. What was he doing?

I'd expected him to come after Olivia, if not immediately, then at least within a day or two, but he hadn't. No one seemed to know where he was.

You should find him. You should talk to him. Remember the way he looked at you at Domingo's wake?

Oh, I remembered. He hadn't been shocked that I was alive and well; no, he'd been furious. Almost as if he'd already known that I wasn't dead.

Perhaps he'd known all this time, in which case...

Why didn't he come for you?

An emotion I didn't recognise shifted in my chest, but I ignored it. I didn't want to go there. Despite all my efforts, Domingo had turned Constantine so completely against me that he'd betrayed Olivia and me without a second's regret. So, of course he wouldn't come for me. Of course he'd only be furious.

That wasn't his fault, though. He'd been a

child, Domingo far too powerful, and I hadn't protected him well enough.

My gut twisted, but I shoved the thoughts away, directing my attention to the financial spreadsheet I had on my computer screen instead.

It was afternoon, and it had been two days since I'd walked out on Olivia.

I hadn't seen her since then, deliberately keeping my distance as I worked through various plans to prove myself worthy of her.

I had options, of course, but none of them were good ones, since they mostly consisted of influencing her in ways she'd no doubt find problematic and not trustworthy in the least.

I was in the process of turning over yet another one, while I fiddled with my spreadsheet, when suddenly the door to my study opened and Olivia came striding in.

She was wearing another of those long, floaty dresses—not that she had a lot of choice, since those dresses were the only clothing in the wardrobe—in dark blue this time with a deep V-neck and long, loose sleeves.

The colour made her skin look like crystal, gave her grey eyes a blue glow and set off her long blonde hair to perfection.

My entire body tightened at the sight of her, desire licking up inside me. It had only been two days, but that had been a long time without her, and my fingers itched to tear that dress off, no matter how lovely it was, and take her right on the floor.

She stopped in front of my desk, folding her arms and lifting her chin.

'Nice to see you, Livvy.' I tried to control the sudden leap of my heart at the sight of her. 'To what do I owe the pleasure?'

'Have you finished sulking, Val?' She gave me an imperious look. 'I'm tired of waiting for an answer. If you're not going to marry me, then where is my plane?'

Delight surged inside me, because I'd missed her. And, *Dios*, how I loved it when she was commanding. It provided me with such a delicious target.

I leaned back in my chair and said lazily, 'Considering you didn't ask for a plane, it's probably still in its hangar.'

Her eyes narrowed. 'I told you I'm not—'

'I missed you,' I interrupted, the truth coming out of me before I could stop it.

She blinked, the imperious look fading, her expression softening. 'You could have come to me at any time. You were the one who walked away, remember?'

And abruptly I was tired of this. Tired of the games. Tired of the fighting. Tired of making plans that didn't work. They weren't getting me what I wanted, and I was done with them.

'Tell me what I need to do, Olivia,' I said honestly. 'Tell me what I need to do to get you to trust me.'

Surprise rippled over her lovely face. 'You want me to trust you?'

I gritted my teeth, not liking that this should come as such a big surprise to her. 'Yes. That's what I said.'

She gave me a long, measuring look. 'Well, not kidnapping me would have been a good start.'

'We've been through that,' I said impatiently.

Tiny sparks leapt in her gaze. And then she was striding up to my desk, slapping her hands down on the top of it and leaning forward, the look on her face blazing now.

'I don't think you understand, Valentin,' she said, abruptly fierce. 'You picked me up and tossed me over your shoulder. You *kidnapped* me. Then you said you weren't sorry about it. And that was *after* letting me believe you were dead for *fifteen years*!' Colour stained her delicate cheekbones and I could see, all of a sudden, the decades-old pain she was hiding. 'You broke my heart. How can you expect me to trust you after all of that?'

There was a wrenching sensation in my chest,

as if there had been an arrow in my heart and she'd just jerked it free. And now I was bleeding, inexplicable pain radiating through me.

You knew what she felt for you. And you hurt her. Everything you've done has hurt her.

'I was trying to save you; don't you see?' My voice had roughened. 'Domingo was still alive, and I was afraid he'd so something to you if I—'

'You think you're the hero of this story, don't you?' she interrupted. 'And I'm just your damsel in distress. You have to save me, and you have to save Constantine, and I don't think for one minute it's about either of us. Because, if it had been, you wouldn't have pulled that ridiculously dramatic stunt with the lights and public announcement.'

She leaned forward a little more. 'You wouldn't have cast me in the role of the helpless victim you need to protect at all costs, taking away my choice by taking me away by force, and then using all my memories of you, the love I once had for you, to make me stay.'

She was breathing very fast now, her eyes glittering. 'You wouldn't have treated me like… like some weak little woman, like your pet or a plaything. And, yes, you could have sent me a damn email. You could have called me. You could have asked me to meet you to talk and we could have gone from there.' She pushed herself away abruptly. 'But you didn't do any of that.'

All the pleasure I'd felt at seeing her had drained away, leaving behind that pain and a hot, defensive anger, both of them demanding an outlet. Demanding I tell her that she was wrong, that she was wrong about all of it. I hadn't treated her like that, and I'd never seen her as some weak little woman, and especially not as a victim.

But you did. You saw her as still that fifteen-year-old girl with no power.

I didn't want to admit she was right. I didn't want to accept that what I'd done hadn't been in her best interests but in mine. Yet the way she'd said it, and the look in her eyes, the pain I could see lurking in the depths…

Your fault.

'I'm sorry,' I said at last, forcing it out. 'I'm sorry for how I treated you. That was the… wrong thing to do.'

But she was having none of it.

'Are you sorry?' she demanded. 'Or would you do it all over again in a heartbeat?'

I gripped the arms of my chair and shoved it back, sending it skittering along the floor as I got to my feet, full of frustrated, directionless rage I didn't understand and didn't know what to do with. 'What more do you want from me,

Olivia? Yes, it was wrong, and I'm sorry. What else do you want me to say?'

'I don't want you to say anything. What I want…' She stopped suddenly and took a breath. 'I'm not your victim, Val. But I'm not your enemy, either. I'm not Domingo and you don't have to fight me.'

Tension gripped me. 'I don't think that.'

'Don't you? Aren't you seeing me as him right now? Him trying to force something from you?'

'No, of course not.' I felt a muscle jump at the side of my jaw. 'No.'

But she only looked at me. 'I'm not trying to prove you wrong. That's not what this is about. You wanted to know what you have to do to get me to trust you—but how I can trust you while I'm still a prisoner on your island?'

CHAPTER FIFTEEN

Olivia

HE STAYED WHERE he was. He wasn't smiling any more, all that lazy charm gone. Now he was angry and defensive, with flames in his eyes.

He was dressed casually again today, jeans and a dark blue T-shirt that deepened his olive-skinned tan and made his eyes and hair look even blacker. The familiar scent of his after-shave wound around me...

I'd missed him these past two days. He was so beautiful, he made me ache.

I'd come in here all set to demand things from him, demand he stop sulking like a little boy and talk to me. Then he'd taken all the wind out of my sails by asking what he needed to do to gain my trust.

At first, I'd thought it was another ploy, but no. He'd been genuine; I'd seen it in his eyes.

So I'd told him and, as soon as I had, all my

hurt and anger had come pouring out. Hurt and anger that had been building ever since he'd walked away from me two days ago. Hurt that he'd walked away in the first place. Anger that I'd been prepared to agree to his offer and yet, for all his insistence, he hadn't.

I'd spent the last two days trying to understand why he'd had such a reaction to my IVF suggestion, and it still didn't make any sense. Because why should he care?

And now he'd completely upended things by talking about trust.

'Why are we talking about this anyway?' I asked when he remained silent. 'You obviously didn't like my answer. So I don't know why my trust should be so important to you now.'

He stood behind his desk, his hands in fists. 'Because I... I want your love, Olivia.' That muscle in his jaw flicked again. 'I told you that. I want us to have what we had all those years ago.'

At first, I didn't understand that either, because why should one teenage relationship be so important to him? Then slowly, as I recognised the intensity that seemed to radiate from every cell of his being, I knew.

He and Constantine had been starved of attention and care by someone who should have given them both. They had been starved of gentleness and kindness—that was why Constantine was so cold and Val so manipulative. Both of them were protecting themselves the only way they knew how. They'd been starved of starved of attention, and most of all they'd been starved of love.

That was what Val wanted, what he was so desperate for. He was an endless pit of need trying to regain that one moment in his life when he'd been loved.

By me.

My eyes prickled, a surge of compassion and sympathy for him swamping me. It hadn't been his fault he'd been so scarred—and he was. I could see it. There were deep fault lines that ran through his soul and had twisted his thinking. His upbringing and the past fifteen years had turned him into a dangerous man, but underneath that he was still that little boy.

A little boy who found pretty shells and driftwood for his study.

A little boy desperate to be loved.

My heart ached for that boy. And it was also aching for the man.

'But we can't have that.' My own sorrow at the knowledge cut deep. 'We can't ever have that again. We were children. And we loved each other as children do.'

He was breathing very fast, staring at me as if

I was his one hope of salvation. 'Then you can leave.' His voice was nothing but deep gravel. 'I'll get you a plane and you can leave. Whenever you want.'

'What?' I blinked in shock. 'Do you mean that?'

'Yes.'

'And what about Constantine?' I couldn't help asking. 'You'll let me marry him if I want to?'

'Yes.'

I searched his face, my heartbeat thudding in my ears, looking for signs that this was another game for him, another way to get me to do what he wanted. Yet… I couldn't see anything in his beautiful features but determination.

He meant it. He would let me go.

The ache behind my breastbone felt abruptly even more painful.

'Why?' I asked huskily. 'After everything you did to get me here?'

His knuckles were white as he held his fists clenched at his sides. 'I don't want you to go. In fact, leaving is the last thing in the world I want you to do. But…if it meant you finally trusting me…then, yes, I'd let you go.' A muscle flicked in his jaw. 'And then I'd send you an email, asking if you wanted to meet me for coffee.'

My throat closed, a surge of some powerful

emotion sweeping through me, and I was trembling, though I wasn't sure why. 'Val…'

'You're not a just thing to me, Olivia,' he said with sudden ferocity. 'You were *never* just a thing. It's true that I wanted the girl you once were, but I want the woman you are now even more.'

I could see the truth in his eyes. He wasn't hiding it, but then he'd never hidden it from me.

His thinking and his motivations might be skewed, but his emotions had always been true.

'What if I don't want to go?' I asked him. 'What if I stayed?'

He didn't hesitate. 'Then we'd have some more dinners. Spend time getting to know one another again. You could swim in the sea, read books, relax in the sun. And, when you were ready, we could discuss our future and whether that would be together.'

I was still shaking. He'd given me something, hadn't he? He'd surrendered something, and now I wanted to do the same.

'My mother was a trophy wife,' I said. 'Dad wanted a son, and she couldn't give him one. He treated her…badly. He didn't respect her; was cruel to her and she just…put up with it. She stayed and I'll never understand why. But one thing I do know is that I won't. I won't put up with being treated the way he treated her, like a thing, like a toy he'd got bored of playing with.'

I swallowed and lifted my chin. 'He treated me like that too until I told him that, if he wanted the family company to stay in the family, he'd have to leave it to me. He respected strength, and so strong is what I always tried to be.'

'Until I took that strength away from you,' Val said with unexpected insight, his black gaze pinned to mine. 'Oh, little star…' He moved then, coming around the side of his desk. But he didn't approach me, standing in front of it instead. 'I gave you no choice. I took you prisoner. I used your own emotions against you…' There was a bleak look in his eyes. 'Did I make you doubt yourself too?'

I wasn't sure how he knew that but…there had been an underlying uneasiness in me that I'd let him do all of this to me. That I hadn't fought hard enough, hadn't stood up to him enough, hadn't challenged him when I should have. That I'd been somehow…weak.

I didn't need to say it, though, because I could see he'd read my expression well enough.

Val muttered a curse under his breath in Spanish. 'You aren't to blame,' he said roughly. 'It was my doing, my responsibility.'

'But I let you—'

'You didn't let me do anything. You slapped me across the face then you pushed me into the sea. You made me work for every concession. You fought me every step of the way.'

I took a breath, not wanting to tell him this, but there seemed little point in not voicing this last doubt. 'I was going to let Constantine pay my debts. I was going to let him take over my company.'

Val took what looked like a helpless step forward before stopping himself, the look on his face blazing. 'First of all, Constantine came to you. And you agreed to his terms because you care about your company and want to save it. You also want heirs, so why not get them from him too? That's not weakness, that's playing the hand your father dealt you which, by the way, wasn't your fault, either.'

That last doubt was one I hadn't even realised was there. That my father's debts were on purpose, one last test for the daughter he'd never really respected.

'Val…' I murmured, suddenly feeling vulnerable.

'Your father was a fool if he couldn't see what he had in you.' Val's voice was full of certainty. 'Strength. Bravery. Passion. You're driven and you're smarter than anyone else I know. But you're not a diamond, Olivia. You're a star, remember? And stars burn.'

I met his gaze at last. Saw the need there, the sheer intensity of it.

He was a star too, wasn't he? A sun, full of rage and love and despair and hope. A difficult, conflicted man, but a man who not only had the ability to take, but the ability to give too. And he wanted to, that was obvious.

So why not let him?

'What do you want, Val?' I asked, knowing that I wasn't going to walk away, not now, not after this.

His dark eyes glittered. 'You. Only you.'

'Then I'll stay.' My breathing had accelerated, my heart beating fast. 'And we'll do all those things you said. On one condition.'

'Anything.' His expression was stripped down, nothing but hunger in it. 'Anything at all, you can have it.'

I took a shaky breath, aware of my own growing need. 'I don't see why sex should be off the table. And so, I'd… I'd like to give you pleasure.'

Surprise flickered over his face, but there was no smile of triumph or satisfaction, only a flare of sexual heat. 'Because you want to? Or because you feel you should?'

He wanted my trust, but trust was a two-way street. And I wanted his too.

So it was me who closed the distance between us, until I was standing right in front of him, and then I reached out to brush his cheek with my fingertips, his skin warm and slightly roughened by his whiskers.

'Because I want to,' I murmured. 'Because you're special to me.'

It felt risky to say it, but I couldn't not. After all, even after all he'd done, it was true.

He stared down at me a moment, his expression impenetrable, then he took my hand from his cheek in a gentle grip and he kissed each one of my fingertips, his mouth warm and velvety. 'Well,' he murmured with a ghost of his old charm. 'Who am I to argue with a lady?'

My heart clenched at the way he kissed my fingers, but I only said, keeping things light, 'Indeed you shouldn't.'

The tension around his mouth eased slightly as he let go of my hand, not so much a smile as an easing of tension. Then he leaned back against the desk. 'Surprise me then, little star.'

So, I did.

My palms were damp as I pulled off the silky dress, my heartbeat loud in my head. I wore nothing underneath it, because I'd been secretly hoping it would end this way between us.

His gaze flared as I let the silk go and it raked down my naked body, lingering in all his favourite places and making me shiver.

'Well?' I asked. 'Are you?'

His attention came back to my face, his smile gone now. 'Surprised? Yes. Yes, I am. You are perfection, Olivia Wintergreen.'

My breathing was fast but I made no attempt to control it and I didn't look away. I let him see the hunger inside me. I let him see the fire as it licked up higher. I let him see it consume me. Because, yes, I burned.

And I wanted him to watch.

I took the last step that separated us, getting close to him, watching the fire catch alight inside him too. 'Don't move,' I whispered.

And he didn't. He stayed exactly where he was, statue-still.

I put a hand to the buttons of his jeans, touching him through the denim, feeling the long, hard shape of him. The breath hissed between his teeth as I mapped him with my fingertips, the flames in his eyes leaping higher. Every part of him was tense, but he didn't move.

He was giving me this by doing what I said. He was giving me his trust. An aching, shifting kind of emotion washed through me then, powerful and familiar, deep and resolute.

His father had controlled and abused him, left

him emotionally isolated with only his brother for company. A brother he'd tried to protect, who'd then betrayed him. He'd been shut in a windowless room for six months and, when he'd finally managed to escape, he'd had to fake his own death just to make sure his father would never find him.

He wasn't scarred on the outside, but he was on the inside.

But he was perfection too and I wanted him to know that.

So I concentrated on what I was doing, tracing him through the fabric of his jeans, stroking him, giving him as much pleasure as he'd given me.

I lifted my hands to his jeans, my fingers now shaking as I undid them. He didn't move, but I could hear his breathing in the silence of the room. It was ragged and short.

I had no idea what I was doing, since I'd never done this to a man before, but somehow that didn't matter. I could see what I was doing to him; he didn't hide it, so I just kept going.

He stayed still as I pulled open his jeans and when I touched him. When I drew him out and held him in my hands. His skin was smooth and hot, and he was so hard.

I leaned forward and traced him with my tongue, tasting him, salt and musk, and he made a soft growling sound that thrilled me right down to the bone.

I took him into my mouth, learning the feel and shape of him, and he made another of those delicious masculine sounds, half-groan, half-growl. His hands were in my hair, not pulling or directing me in any way, just massaging my skull gently before drawing his fingers through the strands, taking a sensual delight in them against his skin.

I glanced up at him, wanting to watch his face as I explored him, using his expressions as my guide, and he didn't look away. He let me see the effect I had on him.

'Livvy...' The words were rough and hot. 'Livvy, you are perfect... Ah, a goddess...'

I loved the husky note in his voice, loved how he hid nothing from me. So I gave him more, gave him hotter and deeper, and he watched me, our gazes connecting, losing ourselves in the fire we were generating between us and being consumed by it.

He growled my name in the end, and pulled my hair, but it didn't hurt, and I liked it. Tasting him had made me even hungrier for him, but I didn't need him to return the favour.

Yet it seemed he had his own ideas about that, because afterwards he helped me to my feet then gripped me, turning round and setting me on top of his desk.

Then he kissed me, long, deep and hard, his hands on my body, stroking me.

I trembled, every part of me alive to his touch. 'You don't have to,' I murmured against his mouth. 'It's not a favour you have to return.'

'I know I don't need to.' His lips brushed over mine. 'But I want to.'

So I let him and, when he found some protection in the top drawer of his desk and dealt with it, sliding inside me at last, all I felt was relief.

I wound my legs around his lean waist and put my arms around his neck, clinging on to him as he moved, a hard, driving rhythm that had me gasping against his mouth. He took me hard and fierce, and it didn't take long before the pleasure inside me burst apart and there were cascading stars everywhere.

'Val,' I whispered against his neck as I shuddered in his arms. 'Oh, Val...'

And, whether I'd said it just for the joy of saying his name, or whether it was a prayer, a request for more or something else, I didn't know.

But it felt as if something had shifted inside me, something momentous.

As if all the barriers had gone and the two halves of my soul had finally become one.

Because of him.

CHAPTER SIXTEEN

Valentin

W<small>E DECIDED TO</small> give ourselves a week.

A week of nothing but long, leisurely dinners on the end of the jetty and lazing about on sun-loungers, diving into the sea when we got too hot. I organised a couple of trips in my yacht, sightseeing around the islands and having picnic lunches on pristine, white sandy beaches.

We talked a lot, catching up on the changes in each other's lives and what we'd been doing for the past fifteen years. I gave her the brutal truth about some of the darker moments in my past, while she confided in me the doubt she had that the Wintergreen board would ever accept her.

It wasn't all plain sailing. We had a minor argument when I tried to insist on no sex, since our chemistry was a powerful force and I couldn't trust myself not to take advantage of it every chance I got. But then she said I was perfectly welcome to use it against her, if she could also use it against me.

Naturally enough, that was an argument that ended in bed, both of us using each other to our mutual satisfaction. And after that, since it was clearly pointless for me to insist otherwise, she'd joined me in my bed every night and we'd explored each other in other ways.

And as the days passed a strange feeling grew in me…something unfamiliar that I couldn't quite describe. Until one day I was watching her swim, her body tanned golden by the sun, and she came up out of the water, naked and dripping wet, and she smiled at me as if I was the best thing she'd seen all day.

And then I realised what the feeling was. Happiness.

It wasn't all sunbathing and sex, of course. We had to deal with Constantine. Olivia had tried contacting him to talk to him, but he remained stubbornly off-grid, so I tried too.

It was frustrating, especially in combination with my continued lack of progress with his lawyers. The will was clear, though. I was the eldest, and therefore everything came to me, which would make removing him as CEO easy.

However, his lawyers continued to stone-wall my efforts to take control. It was true that my former deceased status represented some legal challenges, but I was determined. The company would be mine and Constantine removed for his own good and that of his staff.

Since Constantine wouldn't answer his phone, and my staff was coming up against a lot of dead ends—apparently no one knew where he'd gone—I had to settle for leaving a message on his voicemail, informing him that he was no longer engaged. Olivia and I had decided in one of our talks that, while we weren't quite at marriage yet, she definitely didn't want to remain engaged to him.

We'd discussed what alternatives she could use to help pay Wintergreen's debts that wouldn't involve her giving up her power and, while I had offered some no-strings financial help, I also made it clear she didn't have to take it.

Even though a part of me was desperate to find a way to make her. Yes, my ability to compromise and not take control all the time was still a work in progress.

Then, just as a week had passed, I was supervising deliveries of certain items from the seaplane on the jetty when my phone vibrated.

Staff were carrying bags and boxes from the plane, and I waved them in the direction of the villa as I pulled my phone out of my pocket. I didn't bother looking at the screen to see who it was, hitting the 'answer' button automatically.

'Valentin,' a deep, cold voice said.

My entire body tightened, a pulse of adrenaline going through me.

Constantine.

'Con,' I said, keeping it casual. 'Thought you'd disappeared off the face of the earth.'

'No.'

'Clearly not. I thought you'd forgotten all about me. And not one word about my arrival back from the dead, either. It's almost as if you want to keep that from the media.' I stared over the endless blue of the ocean. 'Oh, and by the way, your lawyers can't stall things for ever. My case is water-tight.'

There was a deep, chilly silence that I found myself listening to intently.

He'd never used to be that silent. Once, he'd been talkative like me. We'd used to tell each other stories when things got bad, about how we'd escape Domingo and what we'd do when we were finally free. Be pirates together, or soldiers. Or cowboys in America.

'The company is mine.' His voice was like ice, reminding me so much of Domingo that I could feel all my muscles tense.

You never wanted that for him. You failed him.

The tight feeling wound around my heart and

I found myself rubbing at my chest before I could stop it. Yes, I knew that. I had. As had Domingo. Domingo had failed us both.

'You know why I'm taking it.' I kept my voice as hard as his. 'It's in the best interests of your company and your staff.'

He ignored me. 'But, if you want Olivia, you can have her.'

'Really?' I struggled to hide my shock. It sounded as if she hadn't meant anything to him at all, which I didn't understand. 'Just like that? You're not even going to make a cursory protest?'

'It was never Olivia that mattered.'

It felt as if I'd been punched in the gut. 'What?'

'I didn't want her.' He sounded as detached as he ever had. 'I never did. What I wanted was my brother. But he made a different choice. So I had to take action.'

The shock deepened inside me and then widened, a freezing lake of it. He wanted…me? But that didn't make any sense. He already had me. And what choice did he mean? I'd never had any choices except the one I'd made to protect him.

'What are you talking about?' I growled. 'What choice? Everything I did back then was for you, you know that.'

'No, it wasn't.' For the first time I could hear

a thread of heat beneath the ice in his voice. 'You chose yourself every single time. You chose that ridiculous feud with Papa.'

'Ridiculous feud?' I echoed in disbelief. 'That man was a—'

'If you'd only obeyed the rules, our lives would have been easier. But you didn't. You made it worse.'

A flash of rage went through me. 'The rules? You think I cared one iota about the rules? You put her life in danger. Domingo told me that, if he caught me seeing her again, he'd do something to hurt her.'

'I did nothing of the sort,' Constantine said icily. 'You were the one who put her in danger, Valentin. It was *your* choice to keep seeing her. If you'd really wanted to protect her, you would have done what our father asked and left her alone.'

He's right.

Well, he was. I knew that already and I'd owned it. Yet ice spiralled through my veins all the same.

I tried to ignore it, gripping tightly to my rage instead. 'I *meant* to disobey him. I was trying to draw his attention away from you, you fool.'

'Yes, that's it exactly.' He sounded frozen, like a glacier. 'You didn't want to let him win. You wanted to prove a point.'

You didn't care about Constantine and you didn't care about her. All that mattered was being stronger than him.

No, that was ridiculous. To have taken all Domingo's manipulative attempts to bring me in line...to have taken all his beatings and his emotional abuse simply to prove I was stronger? What kind of idiot did Constantine take me for?

'You can think that if you like,' I gritted out between my teeth. 'But I was doing all of that for you. I was trying to protect you.'

'I didn't need protecting. And, if you hadn't made things worse, neither would Olivia.'

You've turned him into a victim, the way you turned her into one.

Denial burned like acid inside me. 'So what is this? Are you defending him? After everything he did to us?'

I shouldn't have cared. This had all happened a decade and a half ago, and I knew he hadn't been able to help himself, that Domingo had turned him against me. Nevertheless, a small part of my anger was for him and his betrayal. We'd had no one but each other when we'd been growing up. Domingo had isolated us from everyone, so we had been each other's friends and confidantes. We'd been supposed to stick together no matter what, to look out for each other, because that was what brothers did.

He was my twin, my other half, and even though I knew it hadn't been his fault in the end he'd betrayed me.

'No,' Constantine said as if none of this touched him in any way. 'I'm merely stating facts.'

'So I was just supposed to sit back and watch him beat you to death? Is that what—?'

'I did not call you to talk about what happened fifteen years ago,' he interrupted icily. 'I called to tell you that you are welcome to marry Olivia. I do not care.'

Then he disconnected the call.

For a second I stood there, holding my phone in my hand, hot fury searing me from the inside out.

How dared he? How dared he tell me everything I'd done had been for myself? He was wrong. I'd done it for him, for my little brother. Every single thing.

Is he wrong, though? You liked fighting Domingo. You liked standing up to him. And all the choices you made were because you didn't want to give Domingo the satisfaction of knowing he'd beaten you.

No, that was wrong. That was the *opposite* of what I'd been trying to do.

All those beatings I'd endured, all those punishments. The systematic stripping away of all the things I liked to do, with no friends, no pets. No going outside to climb trees or swim in the huge pool that no one ever used. No games with my brother…

Constantine thought all of that had been so I could *win*?

It hadn't been a competition; didn't he understand that? It had been a fight to the death. It had been me, constantly trying to make sure that Constantine survived.

My brother had always been the kinder of the two us. The more generous, the more giving. He was the one who'd once carefully manoeuvred a bumble bee that had blundered its way inside into a glass and taken it outside rather than kill it. Who'd been inconsolable when we'd discovered a dead kitten under the trees in the garden behind the mansion. And who'd tried unsuccessfully to nurse a sparrow chick that had fallen out of its nest back to health.

His softer emotions had made him an easier target and, since I'd been the one who'd always stood up to Domingo, I had become his shield. Because I hadn't cared about the bee or the kitten or the chick. I'd felt sorry for them, but I hadn't cried the way Constantine had. Domingo had called me the stronger one, and he'd been right, which had made it my duty to protect my little brother.

So I had, and in the end I'd failed. But that was my issue to make right and, even though it was too late for Constantine, it wasn't too late to limit his influence and the damage someone like him could do.

Or is that just you turning yourself into the hero once again?

I growled under my breath. No, that was ridiculous. Perhaps I had done that with Olivia, but not with him. I might have failed him, but I couldn't save him. I could only save the company and the people in it.

Shoving my phone back into my pocket, I dismissed thoughts of my brother and got back to doing something more pleasant.

Being with Olivia.

CHAPTER SEVENTEEN

Olivia

I'D HAD THE most wonderful week. Spending time with Val had been a revelation. It had almost been like those days back on our secret beach, when there'd been only us, only each other.

Except this time it was better, because we were adults now, and our connection was based on reality instead of dreams. And we did have a connection; I could feel it. I could see it in his eyes whenever he looked at me, whenever he touched me, whenever he cupped my face between his large, warm palms and kissed me.

It was a different sort of connection, deeper, more intense. Initially I hadn't liked him taking care of me, because I felt like a plaything or pet, but I gradually saw how much pleasure he took from it. It made him happy to look after my needs. He'd always been protective and care-giving—it was part of his nature—and the pleasure he so obviously got out of it made me happy too. And soon I didn't feel like his plaything but his treasure.

I wasn't sure what would happen when our week of being together came to an end, but I was sure I didn't want to marry Constantine. And maybe, despite my own protests to myself, I'd never wanted to marry him, regardless of those debts.

I discussed the debts with Val and considered other options. Val had offered to lend me some money, because he couldn't help himself and, while I was appreciative, I refused. I wanted to find my own way out of the situation, options that didn't rely on a man's help for a start.

First, though, I needed to contact Constantine to break off our engagement. However, he hadn't responded to my texts or the voicemail messages I'd left on his phone. I didn't know what was happening with him and I couldn't deny I was worried. I didn't love him, but I'd still been engaged to him for three months, and the fact that he seemed to have dropped off the face of the earth was a concern.

But there was still nothing in the media about his disappearance, and certainly shares in Silver Inc were still flying high, which presumably meant no one else was concerned about him.

He was still managing his company, though for how long was anyone's guess.

Val hadn't mentioned his takeover intentions again, but I presumed that was also still going ahead. I'd already told him I didn't like the idea of him removing his brother as CEO, but he seemed firmly wedded to it for reasons I didn't understand. It was a conversation I needed to have with him at some point, but I had other things on my mind.

Over the past couple of days, I'd been pursuing further my idea for sourcing only ethical diamonds. Dad had always paid lip service to the ethical part, but I didn't want lip service. And closer investigation seemed to indicate that the board had been…obscuring a few things when it came to sourcing our gems.

In fact, there were a few things about the board that were suspect. Things that might have had something to do with Dad's financial mismanagement, and that was just downright unacceptable.

Perhaps it was time for a new broom to sweep away the remains of a past that clearly wasn't working. And perhaps it was time for me to be that broom. For too long I'd been trying to do things Dad's way simply so I could prove I could do them better. But maybe I needed to change my approach. Maybe I needed to do things *my* way, not his, and not worry about whether it was too female.

Concern for all employees of Wintergreen and those that supplied us with our precious resources wasn't merely a female thing. It was a human thing. And, just because a few old men didn't like the idea of spending a bit extra to make sure no one was exploited, that didn't mean I couldn't change things.

I was passionate about the business and I'd been reining in that passion for far too long because I hadn't wanted to seem too feminine and upset the board. But Val was right. There was a place for passion in business, and I was going to show them that once and for all. Women were dangerous and those old men had better watch out.

I couldn't wait to share my ideas with him.

I was sitting in the living area, the big glass doors pushed back to let in the cool breeze from the sea, when the sound of the seaplane leaving caught my attention.

I'd idly watched a procession of people carrying all sorts of items, moving along the jetty to the villa and back again, supervised by Val.

I wasn't sure what they were—probably more food, since our supplies were on the low side—but I soon lost interest as my attention caught on Val's tall figure, striding along the jetty as the plane took off behind him, every line of him radiating fury.

I saved the document I was working on and pushed my laptop shut, getting to my feet as Val strode from the jetty to the deck, coming towards the big glass doors. He wore a casual white shirt today instead of a T-shirt, the sleeves rolled up to reveal tanned, powerful forearms. I particularly liked that look on him. It was sexy.

He came through the glass doors and into the room, his anger swirling around him like a hurricane, his eyes full of black fire.

I frowned, concern tightening inside me, and I went over to him, placing my hands on his chest to calm him. 'What's wrong?'

He looked down at me, his expression hard, his jaw tight. 'Apparently, Constantine hasn't dropped off the surface of the earth. I just had a call from him.'

Everything in me went taut. 'Oh? What did he say?'

Val's hands dropped to my hips and he gripped me hard all of a sudden. 'Take off your clothes.' His voice was rough, his eyes glittering. 'I need to let off some steam.'

He was an intensely physical man, I'd discovered, and he'd use either sex or physical exertion to get rid of excess emotion, but I had a feeling that sex wouldn't calm him down this time. Not if it involved his brother.

And this wasn't just anger. This was more.

'Not yet.' I kept my voice cool to counter his heat. 'Tell me what he said, Val. You're upset.'

A muscle leapt in his jaw, his shoulders taut. His expression twisted and I could tell that he wanted to deny it, but he didn't. Instead, his hands dropped and he took a couple of steps back then turned sharply away. He strode over to the big glass doors then stopped, shoving a hand through his black hair.

'He told me I can have you,' he said after a moment. 'But he'll fight me for the company.'

I didn't care if Constantine wanted to let me go. After all, I didn't want him. But I wasn't sure why Val was so angry about it. Was it really just about the company?

'Well, okay,' I said, trying to sound measured. 'You must have known he wouldn't give up the company. And as for me—'

'You don't understand.' Val turned around sharply, the expression on his face blazing with fury. 'He blames me for it. He blames me for *everything*.'

I stared at him, bewildered. 'Blames you for what?'

He dropped his hand from his hair, then turned away again, pacing the length of the room before turning and pacing back again. Anger and frustration poured off him, making my chest ache.

I didn't like seeing him like this. No, I didn't just not like it. I hated it. I wanted to help him, but I didn't know what to do.

'Talk to me, Val.'

'What is there to say?' His black eyes burned, the ghost of his long-lost Spanish accent beginning to colour his words. 'All my life I protected him. He was the one most at risk from Domingo. He had a soft heart, he felt things deeply and that made him an easy target. I was the oldest. I was the strongest. Everything I did was to keep him safe.'

His voice deepened, became rougher, and there was something bleak in his expression. 'It wasn't the beatings that were the worst part, even though they hurt. The worst part was the isolation. He took…everything away. As soon as it looked to him as if you were taking pleasure out of something, he would take it. We couldn't run and play outside, no swimming in the pool or climbing trees. We weren't allowed friends. No dogs, no cats. Constantine had a plastic soldier that one of the housekeepers had given him and he loved it. He played with it a lot and I told him… I told him that it was a bad idea to get attached to it. But he didn't listen.

Then one day Domingo caught him with it and told him to melt it down in the fire.'

He bared his teeth in a facsimile of a smile. 'Constantine was inconsolable and I couldn't stand it. So, I grabbed the solider and ran outside with it, and I threw I it on the roof where Domingo couldn't get it. He beat me half to death that night, but he forgot about that soldier. And that's when I knew what I had to do. I had to keep disobeying him so he'd leave Constantine alone.'

He'd told me some of this over the course of the past week, but not the details. Not about the soldier. Not about Constantine and his soft heart. And I'd been right to think that the scars inside him ran deep. I could see them right now in his eyes.

He was furious, burning up inside with rage.

I wanted to go to him, put my hands on him again, but he was back to pacing, and I didn't want to do anything that might make it worse, so I stayed where I was. 'And you did get his attention,' I said levelly. 'You did keep your brother safe.'

'No, I didn't,' Val growled with a certain amount of savagery. 'I didn't keep him safe, not in the end. I failed him. And Con said I made Domingo worse, that things might not have got as bad as they were if I'd only done what I was told and followed his rules.'

He spat out a harsh curse in Spanish.

'How could I do that, though? Was I supposed to lie down and take it like my mother did?' He stopped, staring out to sea. 'Domingo killed her, I think. In the end, at least. She went for a walk in the mountains and just…never came back. They found a body eventually, at the bottom of a cliff, but I don't believe she fell. I will never believe she fell.'

My heart squeezed, a cold horror winding through me at the thought of two small boys losing the one person who could have protected them or shielded them…

It didn't bear thinking about.

I took a step towards him, wanting to put my arms around him, but stopped. Would he welcome that? I wasn't sure.

He wasn't looking at me but out over the sea, the strangest expression on his face. 'She did whatever he said. She lived her life in fear. And she told me I had to do what he said too, because that was what would keep Con and me safe.'

A muscle flicked in his jaw. 'But it didn't keep her safe, did it?' He turned his head all of a sudden, his gaze colliding with mine, the burning heat in it tearing the breath from my lungs. 'Only I did that. Only I saved him. And you want to know why I think he's every inch Domingo now? Because he told Domingo about our secret beach. About our secret meetings. He put you in danger and he wasn't even sorry about it.'

I heard the note of pain beneath the anger. He'd always been very up-front about his failure with Constantine, and I could see why he believed it. Yet some of it didn't ring true.

He could see me, and I was fine; nothing had happened to me. Plus, all of this had happened fifteen years ago, and Val wasn't a grudge-keeper. He wouldn't be this angry simply because his brother had told on him back when they were teenagers.

No, this went deeper, cut closer to his soul. Something had hurt him, and hurt him terribly. What was it?

This time I went to him without hesitation, coming to stand in front of him. 'Val, tell me. Why are you so angry? Is it just about that?'

'I protected him. That's why I took all the punishments Domingo dealt out. It was so he didn't have to. And I know I failed him. I knew it the moment he went to Domingo about you and me, because he'd never have betrayed me like that if Domingo hadn't got to him. But…' His black eyes glittered. 'I was prepared for him to blame me for not saving him. I wasn't prepared for him telling me I made it worse. That it was all about winning for me. About point scoring. About not giving Domingo the satisfaction of besting me.'

His voice was full of anger, but underneath that anger I heard the doubt.

He wasn't angry because he knew his brother was wrong. He was angry because he was afraid his brother might be right, wasn't he?

'I can't speak for Constantine,' I said. 'He never spoke a word about you or Domingo, or his childhood. But…why are you so intent on getting the company? What are you going to do with it? You don't need to protect Constantine any more and Domingo's dead. What are you trying to prove?'

Val's eyes flashed. 'So, you agree with him, do you? You think this is just about point-scoring too?'

'No, I don't think that. And stop putting words into my mouth.' I kept my cool and stepped closer to him, hoping my presence would help, because now his defence mechanisms were kicking in and they were looking for a target. 'I'm not the enemy, remember? I'm only trying to get to the truth. Who are you angry at—Domingo or Constantine? Or is it more that you're afraid that Constantine was right about you?'

Val lifted his hands and he grabbed me by

the upper arms, not hard, but firmly enough to make me gasp. As if the pressure of his hold could make me see. His mouth twisted in a smile so bitter, it hurt to look at. 'Perhaps he was right. Perhaps it was all just me wanting to prove to my *father*'—he spat the word like it was poison—'that I was everything he thought I was. That I was strong, that I could take everything he threw at me. That I was worthy.' A sneer twisted his mouth. 'Perhaps it was never about protecting Constantine at all, but only about me wanting a psychopath to care.'

I could hear the desperation. That same desperation was in his eyes too.

He was afraid that it was true. That it was *all* true. He'd wanted someone to notice him; he'd wanted someone to care. He'd wanted someone to love him and the only person in his life he could have got that from was his father.

His psychopathic father.

You could give it to him. You could give him everything he needs.

As soon as that thought crossed my mind, I felt something break open inside me, the shell of an egg cracking, a pane of hard diamond shattering, allowing what was inside to come flooding out. An aching, burning, blazing, wondrous thing. Powerful and raw, the white-hot heart of a star...

Everything I'd been keeping inside me for so long. Everything that had been there all this time. Everything I'd known the moment he'd walked into that ballroom in Madrid.

I loved him. I'd always loved him. I'd loved him then and I loved him now and I'd love him for ever. And he needed it. He needed me.

I reached up, took his face between his hands and pulled his mouth down on mine.

CHAPTER EIGHTEEN

Valentin

THE FURY ATE me alive, burning up like a fire inside me. But Olivia's mouth was cool, and suddenly cool was all I wanted.

Cool, to douse all this heat.

I didn't move, taking a moment to get myself in hand, to concentrate on her mouth and the soft touch of her fingers on my face.

Our kisses over the past week had been passionate and intense, but this was different. She didn't open her mouth this time, and she didn't press close to me; she simply cupped my face in her palms and kissed me delicately and without demand. As if the pleasure was all in my lips on hers and she'd be satisfied with that and nothing more.

I was impatient, though, and as suddenly as I wanted cool I wanted heat instead, and fire, channelling my own pointless fury into sex, which was the most pleasurable way to channel the emotions I didn't want.

I didn't want this fury. I didn't want Olivia looking at me as if she knew exactly what I was thinking, which she didn't.

She'd never had to deal with Domingo.

She didn't know what it was like to want the attention of a psychopath. To enjoy it. To like matching wits with him, to like standing up to him. To be pleased to see respect and approval in his eyes.

To know that all this time you'd been telling yourself lies about how you were trying to protect your own brother, about how you were the hero, when all along you were so desperate for your father's approval, you didn't care what you had to do to get it.

And you still don't care. You don't care that you took her away by force. You don't care that you're going to take Constantine's company from him like you took away his toy soldier. You dress it all up by telling yourself you're protecting them, but you're not. You're not the hero. You're the villain.

I reached for Olivia, jerking her close, trying to drown that thought in the sweet taste of her mouth. Drown all the terrible doubts that pulled inside me. The fear that, yes, I had made it worse for Constantine with my constant rebellions and defiance. And, yes, my choice to disobey Domingo had put Olivia in harm's way.

And maybe even something I'd done had led to my mother's death…

What if it did? You hurt people and you don't care about them. You only care about yourself.

Her hands were stroking me, my racing thoughts fracturing beneath her fingers, and abruptly I was desperate.

I needed to get rid of the voice in my head; I needed her and the pleasure she gave me to strip it away.

My hands tightened on her hips and I walked her back to the couch. Then I pushed her down onto it, raking up the thin silk of her dress.

She welcomed me as she always did, her legs wrapping around my hips, the damp heat between her thighs pressing against my fly. 'Slow down,' she whispered in my ear, her hands gently stroking. 'There's no rush.'

But I didn't want slow. I didn't want gentle. I wanted oblivion.

I shifted onto my knees between her spread legs and reached down, tearing the fabric of her dress completely apart. She was naked beneath it as during the past week she hadn't bothered with a bikini.

Her body was beautiful, her pale skin lightly tanned after a few days of swimming naked in the sun. She was perfect, so perfect. I reached down to undo my fly, but she sat up, her hands covering mine. Her eyes were full of heat and something else, something I couldn't read. It looked like tenderness or sympathy, or maybe even pity, and I didn't like it.

'Don't look at me like that.' I growled. 'Just lie down.'

'Don't look at you like what?' Her hands had found their way under the hem of my shirt, her cool fingers stroking my stomach. But the look in her eyes wasn't cool. It blazed with increasing intensity. There was no trace of her veneer, no trace of the diamond armour she wore.

But she wasn't purely the girl I remembered from years ago, either. She was more. She was strength and vulnerability and passion all at once.

She was a star. A pure, glorious star. 'Don't look at you like I love you?'

It shouldn't have been a shock to hear those words. It should have been something expected, because wasn't that the whole point of this mission? To get her to love me the way she had when she was fifteen?

She'd said those words to me once before, as we'd lain under the stars on our beach. And I'd said them back. I'd never had anyone love me or tell me so before, not even Constantine, because why would he? He'd had no idea what those words meant, and neither had I. Not until her.

So this moment should have been triumphant; it should have been a win.

Yet it wasn't triumph that settled in my gut, but ice.

You kidnapped her. You manipulated her to get what you want. Everything you do is about what you *want. And now you have it. You have everything.*

The words filled my head, I couldn't stop them.

This was what I'd wanted all this time, yet… the only reason she'd said it was because I'd brought her here and forced her to deal with me. So…was it even real? If I'd sent her that email instead, met her for coffee like I'd told her that day in my office, would she have loved me then? Without me kidnapping her and manipulating her with our past? When it had just been me?

Of course she wouldn't. Why would she want someone like you?

Her eyes were so clear, so beautiful. 'Because it's true, Val. I love you. I don't think I ever stopped loving you.'

The cold spread inside me, deepening.

Psychopaths have no empathy. They don't care about anyone but themselves. You're the

*villain, remember? It's not Constantine who's
exactly like him. It's you.*

The cold became ice.

I pushed myself away from her, my heart
freezing solid.

'Val?'

I got off the couch and took a couple of steps
away from it, turning my back on her, trying to
get myself together.

'Val?' Soft arms wound around me, her
warmth against my back. 'I'm sorry. Should I
not have said that?'

I stared at the blue sky and the blue sea. It
was beautiful, so warm, and yet all I could feel
was the darkness inside me. The darkness that
had always been there, that I'd done anything
and everything to deny.

But I couldn't escape it and I never would.

Constantine wasn't the psychopath.

The psychopath was me.

CHAPTER NINETEEN

Olivia

THE EXPRESSION ON Val's face was like ice. I'd never seen him so cold. He looked almost exactly like Constantine.

I'd only wanted to give him what he needed, the love he was so obviously craving, because if ever a man needed love it was this one. But he'd acted as if I'd stabbed him and I didn't know why.

I wasn't going to take it back, though. I could pretend I hadn't said it, retreat behind my armour, change the subject or walk away, but... I couldn't do any of those things.

He was too important.

'It's true, you know,' I said. 'I love you. And I'm not sorry I said it.'

He moved out of my embrace, pacing a few feet away. 'You shouldn't.' There was frost in his voice. He sounded just like his brother now, complete with that sexy accent. 'Because I don't think you quite understand what you're dealing with.'

I quelled the urge to go to him again and wrap my arms around him. 'What do you mean?'

His black eyes glittered strangely. 'Psychopaths don't care about other people. They have no empathy. Other people's feelings don't matter to them in the slightest.'

'Domingo's dead. He's got nothing to—'

'Is he dead?' Val smiled all of a sudden, and it was a terrible smile. 'Or is he still here? Is he standing right in front of you?'

I blinked, my mouth going dry. 'Oh, Val, no. That's not—'

'I liked it. Did you know that?' He said it almost conversationally. 'I liked fighting with him. I liked challenging him. I enjoyed it. I liked the attention.' He kept on smiling that bitter smile. 'I wasn't kind like Constantine. I didn't cry about dead kittens and didn't care about that bird. I just wanted to win.' He met my gaze. 'Like he did.'

'No.' I made the word hard, flat with denial, because I knew what he was going to say next. 'You're not like him. You're not.'

'Aren't I? Domingo knew how to charm, to get people to think he was just a normal man. He knew how to manipulate them to get what he wanted. And he took what he wanted without thought. Doesn't that sound familiar to you?'

He did. He did think that. He thought he was the same.

My heart kicked, aching for him. Because it wasn't true. It had *never* been true. He was flawed, yes, and he was scarred too, but Valentin Silvera wasn't his father. And it wasn't true that he didn't care. He *did* care. He cared too much.

'No,' I said again. 'You're *not* him. You're *nothing* like him.'

'You really don't think so? And don't take the fact that I didn't hurt you as a sign. Because he didn't use physical force against people, not for the most part. Even with us, he didn't beat us often. He used our emotions against us; that was his favourite method.' Val's gaze went straight through me. 'The way I used yours.'

I moved closer to him, wanting him to understand. 'You're angry. You're angry at what he did to you, that's all. And anger doesn't come from nowhere. If you didn't care then, yes, I might be worried, but that's not the case. You do care. You care deeply and you're furious about it.'

But it was clear he wasn't listening.

'Did I care about you, though, Olivia? Did I even care for Constantine? I planned to take his company from him, and do you think I ever thought for one moment about how he might feel? And you? What about you? I didn't care when I threw you over my shoulder. I didn't even think about you. I was only thinking about myself.'

Bitter fury coloured his words. 'You told me I'd cast myself as the hero of the piece, and you're right. I did. I told myself I was making up for my failure by taking Constantine's company, that it was for his own good. And that I was saving you from him too.' He shook his head. 'But what if it isn't? What if all I'm doing is taking what I want because I want it? Because I can? Because it's fun.'

His expression was so bleak, my heart squeezed tight with pain. 'I'm not the hero, Olivia. I'm the villain.'

I looked at him, looked deep into his eyes, and beneath that bitterness I saw the pain. I could see, too, why he thought those things about himself. Maybe, a couple of weeks ago, I would even have agreed with him.

But I didn't agree now. Yes, his methods had been selfish and manipulative, but he'd listened to me when I'd called him on them. He'd apologised and been genuine about it. He'd asked me what I wanted, and what he could do to earn my trust, and then he'd gone about doing it.

But, more than anything else, this whole time he'd uncovered some of my own demons and helped lay them to rest. He'd helped me realise that I didn't have to be so hard and so cold. That I didn't have to hold myself back, that passion was allowed.

'You're not a villain.' I put every ounce of belief in my voice. 'And you didn't do any of that for fun. I think you did it because you're still angry at your father and you're trying to get back at him.'

'But how do you know I'm not using that to manipulate you right how?' He smiled and this time there was nothing bitter about it. It was all charm. 'How can you ever know if anything I do is real or genuine?'

I just looked at him. 'Like you're manipulating me right now? Trying to scare me away? No, Val. I know when you're genuine. Because I know you. And I trust you.'

Pain flickered over his face and I saw that change in his eyes, the shift. 'Except you can't, little star. You can't ever trust me. How can you, when I don't even trust myself?'

I had some premonition then, a certainty that gripped me. 'Don't,' I began.

But he didn't let me finish. 'You need to leave, Olivia,' he said gently. 'You should go back to

Madrid. Tell Constantine you've changed your mind. Marry him.'

Of course he'd push me away.

Of course he'd want me to leave.

A bone-deep ache settled down inside me. 'You really want me to do that? You really want me to leave you?'

His expression had hardened. 'You can't stay. I won't let you. I'll only break your heart again, and you know it.'

I lifted my chin. 'Maybe, but isn't that my choice to make?'

'So, what? You'll stay with a man who doesn't even know what love is, let alone how to express it?'

The ache settled deeper inside me, because I could see that he truly believed that. And that I hadn't had long enough to teach him to believe otherwise. He didn't trust me, and he didn't trust himself, and I didn't know what to do.

He was a difficult man, scarred by his terrible childhood. But his instinct had always been to protect, no matter what he told himself about his battles with his father. He'd wanted to protect his brother; that was certain. And he'd wanted to protect me too. Those feelings had been genuine.

His heart was true.

'So that's it?' I demanded, suddenly furious

myself. 'After everything we've been through, you just give up?' I strode over to him, giving him a taste of the passion and fire that lived inside me. 'It's because it's easier, isn't it? Easier to believe you're just like Domingo than it is to accept that I might love you. That I might want to be with you, to marry you instead. And I do, Val. You asked me a while ago what it was that I wanted, and I know now. It's you. I want you.'

Val stared at me, his eyes black flames. 'You don't know what you're talking about, Olivia. Your feelings… They're not real.'

But I didn't back down. 'Don't you dare tell me about my feelings, Valentin Silvera.'

'So if I'd come to you cap in hand in Madrid? Asked you out for coffee? What would you have done? You'd have turned around and walked away. The only reason you think you love me now is because I forced you to come here with me.'

I came closer, standing right in front of him, looking up into his eyes, trying to see where he was coming from him, trying to read him, and…he was afraid, wasn't he? He was afraid to take what I was giving him, because he didn't trust me.

I trusted him, but he didn't trust me.

And maybe he never would.

Maybe he'd never be able to give me that,

never lower his defences enough to let me in. Maybe he was too scarred, too broken.

Maybe I'd end up just like my mother, staying with a man who didn't love her. Convincing herself that one day she'd change his mind and yet knowing it was never going to happen. Because she wasn't enough for him, just as I'd never been enough for him.

I could feel pain setting in, my heart fracturing along the same lines as it had years before, because the only option I had was doing the same thing she had: spending my life with a man who would never give me what I truly wanted.

His heart.

Except, that's not quite true, is it?

I blinked. Wasn't it, though? Love, as he'd said, wasn't something he knew anything about.

But I did. And so…why was I afraid? Wasn't my heart big enough for both of us? Wasn't I strong enough to deal with him? And why did I think I'd end up like my mother? Because I wouldn't. I would always challenge him, stand up to him. I'd never let him walk all over me. And that wasn't even what I'd been afraid of all this time—I knew that now.

It was love that had scared me. Love had broken me at fifteen and I hadn't wanted ever to go near it again. But I was different now, stronger.

And, strangely, I wasn't afraid. There was only that white-hot heart of the star burning inside my chest. A fire that would never go out, that would burn hot and powerful.

Love was that fire, and it wasn't a weakness or a flaw. It was a strength. A power.

I stared at Val, let my love for him blaze in my eyes so he would know what it looked like, so he would recognise it.

'You're wrong,' I said. 'You haven't forced me to love you. You only uncovered what was already there. I loved you then, Valentin Silvera, and I love you now. And, if you think I'm walking away from you, you can think again.' I paused, giving him a fierce look. 'I don't care how long it takes. You will be mine eventually. Count on it.'

Then I turned and went over to the couch and picked up the ripped shreds of my dress, draping them casually over my shoulder. 'Well,' I went on calmly. 'It's a lovely day and this is a lovely island. And I've just realised it's been a long time since I've taken a holiday. So… I think I'll stay here for a week or two. If you don't mind, that is.'

His face darkened and he took a step forward. 'Olivia, don't—'

'Don't what? You wanted me to choose, Val, so I'm choosing. And I choose to stay.' I

strolled over to the door that led to the hallway
and tossed him a smile over my shoulder. 'After
all, I could do with a holiday.'

And, before he could reply, I walked out.

CHAPTER TWENTY

Valentin

I DIDN'T UNDERSTAND why she wanted to stay. After I'd taken everything from her. After I'd kidnapped her. Manipulated her into sex. Used her the way I'd used my brother, all to satisfy my own wants and needs.

To satisfy my anger towards a man who was dead.

A man I'd never called Father and yet for some reason a man I'd wanted attention from all the same.

I'd hated him. I'd thought it was Constantine who was like him, not me.

But I'd been wrong. All this time, I'd been wrong.

I let her walk out and I didn't follow, because what could I say? I couldn't love her the way she deserved to be loved. How could I? I'd thought I knew what love was, but I didn't. Another thing I'd been wrong about.

The rest of the day I tried to lose myself in work, but I couldn't concentrate, so I lost myself in exercise instead, trying to outrun the realisation that had frozen me down to my soul.

For once, I felt nothing. My anger was gone; the intense feelings of desire and hunger had vanished.

I'd become my father at long last.

Night came swiftly, as it did in the tropics, and that was when I saw it—the flames of a driftwood fire on the beach.

It was her; of course it was her.

I ignored her for as long as possible and then, when I couldn't any more, I found myself striding down the jetty towards that fire. I'd tell her to put it out, that was what I'd do, and then I'd walk away. Because, if she wasn't going to, I would. I'd take the first plane out and go back to Europe. Find my brother. Take his company.

I should certainly have felt something about that, some kind of triumph at least, but my heart felt dead inside me. As if a light had gone out.

I was a frozen wasteland.

I found her sitting on a blanket she'd spread over the sand wearing only a silky loose white top through which I could see the delicate little bikini she wore underneath. Her hair was down over her shoulders and she smiled when she saw me, her face lighting up.

The way mine had lit up when I'd seen her for the first time all those years ago.

My chest ached, the ice inside me shifting.

'Come and sit down.' She patted the blanket beside her then picked up a bag of something on the other side of her and waved it at me. 'I've got marshmallows.'

The shifting feeling in my chest deepened into pain.

She must have found those marshmallows in the kitchen, because I'd got them for exactly this reason. To toast them over the driftwood fire the way we'd done all those years ago.

'You need to put the fire out,' I ordered.

'Do I?' She frowned. 'I don't see why. Nothing's going to catch alight.' She picked up a sharpened stick. 'Come on, sit with me. You know I can't do toasted marshmallows as well as you.'

It was true, she never could. I was the best.

The pain began to radiate outwards from inside me and I didn't want it. I wanted the deadness back.

Of course you do. But that's the easy way out, isn't it? If your heart is dead, you can't feel pain.

That was true. Just as if you didn't care, you couldn't be angry.

'If you didn't care then, yes, I might be worried, but that's not the case. You do care. You care deeply and you're furious about it.'

That was what she'd said to me this morning, her gaze direct. As if she'd seen something in me, something that I knew wasn't there.

The pain intensified, because I wanted it to be there.

I wanted to sit next to her. I wanted to toast the best marshmallow and then I wanted to feed it to her. I wanted to have her warm, bare thigh next to mine, and I wanted to talk about foolish things that made us both laugh.

I wanted to give her an engagement ring and see her in a wedding dress.

I wanted to marry her.

I wanted to spend my life with her.

But how could I do that? How could I ask her to marry a man like me? A man who'd been lying to himself all this time about who he was. A man who couldn't even trust himself.

A man who didn't know, who didn't understand, what the word love meant.

I couldn't ask that of her. I couldn't. It would be repeating what her own parents' marriage had been like and I couldn't do that.

She was a star that burned and I… I was nothing but ash.

I turned to go, to head back to the villa, but then I heard her voice.

'Don't go,' she said softly. 'Please stay.'

And I stopped in my tracks. Because those were the words I'd said to her that day on the beach when I'd met her. She'd been so cross to see me and I'd known she was going to leave. I hadn't wanted her to. I'd been desperate for her to stay.

And she had. She hadn't left me. She hadn't left me alone.

A bolt of something hot pulsed down my spine in that moment like lightning, rooting me to the spot.

I didn't know what was happening, but I could feel things shifting around inside me, re-arranging themselves into a different shape, a picture I couldn't quite see yet.

I didn't turn, didn't want to move in case I disturbed that picture coming into view, but it was still distorted, still blurry.

'Why are you still here?' I demanded, staring out over the water, impatient because it was just within reach, that picture, but I still couldn't see it. 'What do you want from me?'

There was a moment of silence behind me, nothing but the crackle of the fire filling the air.

'I want you to trust me, Val,' Olivia said softly. 'I know it's hard after what Domingo did to you. I know it's hard to trust anyone. But you can trust me. And you can trust my love for you. That's why I'm still here. I meant what I said. I'm not leaving.'

My anger turned inside me, the frozen wasteland melting.

I wanted to deny that Domingo had done anything to me, but I couldn't. He'd twisted me just as thoroughly as he'd twisted Constantine.

'You think that's easy?' I demanded.

'No.' She sounded very calm. 'I think it's the most difficult thing in the world. It's a leap of faith, Val. But if you never take it, all you're doing is letting your father win.' She paused. 'You never let him win before, my love. Why start now?'

My heart was suddenly hammering in my chest and I couldn't breathe. It was almost as if I was afraid.

'I don't know how to do this,' I found myself saying, my voice hoarse. 'I don't know how to love you. I don't even know if I can.'

'Of course you can,' she said simply. 'You gave me laughter and honesty and belief. You gave me courage. You gave me the strength to be who I am. To embrace it and not be afraid. And what's that if not love?' Another pause. 'I think it's time for you to do the same.'

I couldn't breathe all of a sudden.

I turned around and stared at her, sitting by the fire, watching me steadily through the flames.

Her mouth curved. 'You're proud and bossy and far too arrogant. And you don't like the word no. But you're also protective and passionate. Gentle too, and never cruel. You have so much love to give, I can feel it, I can see it. And you want someone to love you too.'

Slowly she rose to her feet, the breeze catching the hem of her tunic and making it float out behind her. 'You're a difficult man, Valentin Silvera, but you're not a difficult man to love. So, come and sit by me and toast me a marshmallow, and then perhaps make love to me under the stars. We could argue after that about the best way to start a fire, perhaps. Or we could simply go back to the villa and I could show you all the ways I love you.'

She smiled, her face lit up by the fire, every part of her shining. My little star. 'Then maybe we'll get married the way we always said we would.'

I stared at her, my heart cracking inside my chest. 'How can you say all these things after everything I did? I let you believe I was dead. I kidnapped you. I—'

'You showed me how it felt to be loved.'

I was shaking.

A leap of faith...

Suddenly I was walking towards the fire, barely conscious of what I was doing. The sand beneath my feet was still warm from the hot day's sun as I skirted the fire, coming to stand in front of her where she stood.

'Show me,' I demanded, every part of me aching and raw. 'Show me what it feels like.'

'Idiot,' Olivia said gently. 'It feels like this.' She reached up and wound her arms around my neck, then pressed her mouth to mine.

And, just like that, the picture snapped into complete, sharp focus.

I did know. I *did* know what love felt like.

Love was sitting on a beach throwing shells even when she was angry with me.

Love was arguing with me about building a fire and then letting me sit by it while we toasted marshmallows.

Love was pushing me off a rock and then laughing when I pulled her in.

Love was a first kiss under the stars and wild passion in the sand and her face glowing as she talked about what she wanted for her company and the gentleness of her fingertips on my jaw.

Love was her sitting by a fire with a bag of marshmallows.

Love was my little star, my Olivia.

You can trust her. Of all the people in the whole world, you can trust her.

A shudder went through me, ice melting under the heat of the sun, and somewhere deep inside I felt part of me let the ghost of my father go.

And then I was wrapping my arms around her, holding her tight, kissing her desperately, kissing her as if I was suffocating and she had all my air.

'Livvy,' I whispered when I could finally breathe again. 'I don't know if I can do this. I don't want to hurt you. I don't want to disappoint you. And I'm afraid I'll end up doing both.'

She looked up at me, her eyes shining. 'Oh, you probably will. And I'll probably do the same to you. No relationship is perfect.'

My heart was pounding. I wasn't sure if this was real. 'But I—'

She cupped the side of my face with one small hand. 'It's scary and, believe me, I'm scared too. But we'll make this work because I love you and that's all that matters.'

She was right. Love *was* all that mattered. And right then and there I decided I would do everything in my power to keep her here with me, to make her happy. And not for myself, but for her.

Because I loved her.

I cupped her face between my palms and

looked down into her beautiful face. 'I love you, Olivia Wintergreen,' I said, and I made a vow. 'And I will spend the rest of my life arguing with you about the best way to start a fire, toasting you the perfect marshmallow, not getting angry when you push me off a rock, making love to you under the stars and trying to make you happy for the rest of my life.'

I took a breath. 'Will you live with me and have my children? Will you marry me?'

Her face blazed, her eyes the white-hot heart of a star. 'Yes,' she said. 'Yes, I will.' And then she kissed me and I caught fire with her.

And, even all these years later, we're still burning.

EPILOGUE

Olivia

MY WEDDING DRESS was perfect—white silk in a wraparound style with a sexy slit that went all the way up to my thigh. My hair was loose and I carried some tropical flowers in a small bouquet.

On my finger was the engagement ring Val had bought me, which I adored. A red diamond. The world's rarest diamond colour. Because I too was rare and beautiful and precious, he'd said, and the red was for passion.

He waited for me at the end of the jetty, dressed all in black, and he watched me with all the ferocious intensity a man like him was capable of. Which was considerable.

My Val.

We'd tried to get hold of Constantine the night before, because Val had decided Constantine could keep his company. Val didn't want it. The only thing he'd ever wanted was me.

And all I'd ever wanted was him.

We were married on the end of the jetty and, when I was finally his wife, his kiss just about burned me alive.

So I pushed him into the sea.

Of course he pulled me in after him, but I didn't mind.

Nothing was going to cool the heat between us, and I didn't want it to.

We would burn together until the end of time.

Because it wasn't just me who was a star.

He was too.

* * * * *

Enchanted by A Diamond for
My Forbidden Bride*?*
Look out for the next sizzling instalment in the
Rival Billionaire Tycoons duet, coming soon.

And don't forget to check out these other
Jackie Ashenden stories!

The World's Most Notorious Greek
The Innocent Carrying His Legacy
The Wedding Night They Never Had
Pregnant by the Wrong Prince
The Innocent's One-Night Proposal

Available now!